THE DUMMY MEETS THE MUMMY!

GOOSEBUMPS®
HALL OF HORRORS

#1 CLAWS!
#2 NIGHT OF THE GIANT EVERYTHING
#3 SPECIAL EDITION: THE FIVE MASKS OF DR. SCREEM
#4 WHY I QUIT ZOMBIE SCHOOL
#5 DON'T SCREAM!
#6 THE BIRTHDAY PARTY OF NO RETURN

GOOSEBUMPS®
MOST WANTED

#1 PLANET OF THE LAWN GNOMES
#2 SON OF SLAPPY
#3 HOW I MET MY MONSTER
#4 FRANKENSTEIN'S DOG
#5 DR. MANIAC WILL SEE YOU NOW
#6 CREATURE TEACHER: FINAL EXAM
#7 A NIGHTMARE ON CLOWN STREET
#8 NIGHT OF THE PUPPET PEOPLE
#9 HERE COMES THE SHAGGEDY
#10 THE LIZARD OF OZ

SPECIAL EDITION #1 ZOMBIE HALLOWEEN
SPECIAL EDITION #2 THE 12 SCREAMS OF CHRISTMAS
SPECIAL EDITION #3 TRICK OR TRAP
SPECIAL EDITION #4 THE HAUNTER

GOOSEBUMPS®
SLAPPYWORLD

#1 SLAPPY BIRTHDAY TO YOU
#2 ATTACK OF THE JACK!
#3 I AM SLAPPY'S EVIL TWIN
#4 PLEASE DO NOT FEED THE WEIRDO
#5 ESCAPE FROM SHUDDER MANSION
#6 THE GHOST OF SLAPPY
#7 IT'S ALIVE! IT'S ALIVE!

GOOSEBUMPS®

Also available as ebooks

NIGHT OF THE LIVING DUMMY
DEEP TROUBLE
MONSTER BLOOD
THE HAUNTED MASK
ONE DAY AT HORRORLAND
THE CURSE OF THE MUMMY'S TOMB
BE CAREFUL WHAT YOU WISH FOR
SAY CHEESE AND DIE!
THE HORROR AT CAMP JELLYJAM
HOW I GOT MY SHRUNKEN HEAD
THE WEREWOLF OF FEVER SWAMP
A NIGHT IN TERROR TOWER
WELCOME TO DEAD HOUSE
WELCOME TO CAMP NIGHTMARE
GHOST BEACH
THE SCARECROW WALKS AT MIDNIGHT
YOU CAN'T SCARE ME!
RETURN OF THE MUMMY
REVENGE OF THE LAWN GNOMES
PHANTOM OF THE AUDITORIUM
VAMPIRE BREATH
STAY OUT OF THE BASEMENT
A SHOCKER ON SHOCK STREET
LET'S GET INVISIBLE!
NIGHT OF THE LIVING DUMMY 2
NIGHT OF THE LIVING DUMMY 3
THE ABOMINABLE SNOWMAN OF PASADENA
THE BLOB THAT ATE EVERYONE
THE GHOST NEXT DOOR
THE HAUNTED CAR
ATTACK OF THE GRAVEYARD GHOULS
PLEASE DON'T FEED THE VAMPIRE
THE HEADLESS GHOST
THE HAUNTED MASK 2
BRIDE OF THE LIVING DUMMY
ATTACK OF THE JACK-O'-LANTERNS

ALSO AVAILABLE:

IT CAME FROM OHIO!: MY LIFE AS A WRITER by R.L. Stine

THE DUMMY MEETS THE MUMMY!

R.L. STINE

SCHOLASTIC INC.

Goosebumps book series created by Parachute Press, Inc.
Copyright © 2019 by Scholastic Inc.

ISBN 978-1-338-22305-7

10 9 8 7 6 5 4 3 2 1   19 20 21 22 23

Printed in the U.S.A.   40
First printing 2019

SLAPPY HERE, EVERYONE.

Welcome to My World.

Yes, it's *SlappyWorld*—you're only *screaming* in it! Hahahaha!

Are you wearing sunglasses? You should. I'm so bright, the sun hides when I come out! Hahaha. I'm so bright, I glow in the dark!

How smart am I? Even though I don't know you, I can spell your name.

Are you ready?

Y-O-U-R N-A-M-E! Hahaha!

Do you know my favorite national holiday? It's *my* BIRTHDAY. Everyone likes to come to my birthday parties because my parties are a SCREAM. Hahaha.

Know my favorite birthday present of all time? It was a pony.

It was DELICIOUS! Hahahaha!

I have a story to tell you, and it takes place in a museum. Did you ever see my picture in the

National Dummy Museum? Of *course* not! Don't call me dummy, Dummy!

But I do belong in a museum. That's because people like to stare at me and admire my good looks. I'm so handsome, every time I peek in a mirror, the mirror says, "Thank you!" Hahaha.

Well, the museum in this story is a haunted museum. And three guesses who haunts it!

I call the story *The Dummy Meets the Mummy!* It's a very creepy mummy story. I think you'll get *all wrapped up* in it! Hahaha!

How did I end up in a haunted horror museum? And why did I have to do battle with an ancient, angry mummy?

You'd better start reading or you'll never find out! Hahaha!

Believe it or not, the story starts at an ancient mummy's tomb in Egypt. And then it gets so scary, you may want to call *your* mummy! *Hahahaha.*

It's just one more terrifying tale from *SlappyWorld.*

PART ONE
CAIRO, EGYPT

1

Dr. Richard Klopfer gazed at his mobile phone. He smiled at the face of his son, Christopher, on the screen. Dr. Klopfer leaned forward in his armchair to talk to him.

Outside the hotel window, he heard car horns honking, a rumble of traffic, voices speaking loudly in Arabic and French and English. A crowded Cairo street.

"I will bring you with me next time, Christopher," he said. He tugged at the sides of his wide salt-and-pepper mustache. "This mission is far too dangerous for a ten-year-old."

"Why is it dangerous?" Christopher demanded. "You're going into an old tomb, and you're going to open up a mummy case and discover another mummy."

"This one is different," Klopfer explained. "The tomb has never been opened because people are too afraid to go inside it."

Christopher squinted at his father. "Afraid?"

5

"Some kind of curse," Klopfer said. He chuckled. "There's always some kind of curse. People believe the weirdest stories. Even in this modern day and age."

Klopfer saw a look of fear cross Christopher's face. "Dad . . . are you going to be okay?"

"Of course!" Klopfer cried. "I'm a scientist. I don't believe in curses. I'm not afraid to go into that tomb."

"Then why didn't you bring me?" Christopher asked.

Before Klopfer could answer, Bella Wortham, his assistant, entered the hotel room. Dr. Klopfer said a quick good-bye to his son and set his phone down on the table.

"Dr. Klopfer, the man from the Egyptian Science Council is here," Wortham said.

"Does he have a worried look on his face?" Klopfer asked her.

She nodded. "Very worried."

Klopfer tugged at his mustache. "I thought so. Send him in, Bella."

Wortham brought the man into the room. "Dr. Klopfer, this is Mr. Amari," she said.

Amari removed his white fedora as he entered and forced a smile to his face. He had black hair, slicked straight back, and dark eyes that studied Dr. Klopfer. He wore a white suit, slightly wrinkled and baggy, with a narrow black tie over his white shirt.

6

He gave Dr. Klopfer a short bow, then reached to shake hands. Klopfer motioned to the chair across from him. Amari sat down and placed his hat on the table.

"You know why I have come," Amari said in a soft voice. "To ask you—"

Klopfer raised a hand. "Please."

"To ask you not to go into the Tomb of Arragotus," Amari finished his sentence. "The tomb has not been disturbed in any way for five thousand years. And there is a good reason."

"Can I offer you something to drink?" Klopfer said. "I could call up for some snacks."

"You are ignoring me," Amari replied, his voice still a murmur.

"Yes," Klopfer agreed. "I am ignoring you, Mr. Amari. I plan to go into that tomb tomorrow and open the mummy case and see Prince Arragotus. I plan to be the first ever to see his remains."

"He was never a prince," Amari said. He picked up his hat and twirled it in his lap between his hands. "You know the story very well. Arragotus was about to be crowned prince. And he was murdered on the morning of his crowning. He never sat on the throne he deserved."

"I've read all that," Klopfer replied. "I still don't believe in the curse."

"He's angry. I'm warning you." Amari grabbed Klopfer's shirtsleeve. "He has not rested. Yes, he is a mummy. But that has not stilled his anger.

He is a mummy who would like to take his revenge."

Klopfer shook his head. "You have watched too many horror movies, sir. That story may frighten children, but I am a scientist. I plan to take Arragotus home to Chicago and study him at great length. He will be famous. He may be angry as you say. But he will still be dead."

Amari rose to his feet. "His remains should not be disturbed. Is there nothing I can say to convince—?"

Klopfer shook his head. "No. But it was kind of you to come, Mr. Amari. I do appreciate your warning."

Amari pushed his hat onto his head. "If you insist on disturbing Arragotus tomorrow, there is only one more thing I can say." He paused. Then he murmured, "Good luck."

The tall pyramid-shaped tomb cast a long shadow over the desert sands. Klopfer and his team arrived in a caravan of jeeps. They parked in a line near the narrow entrance, a low, dark cave opening.

The entrance and the tunnel inside the ancient tomb had taken two years to dig. And now Klopfer's heart beat with excitement. He was finally going to see the mummy. He was finally going to achieve his dream.

The local guards went in first to make sure the tunnel was clear and safe. The video crew went next. Klopfer wanted every second of his triumph to be seen by the world.

Then Klopfer led the way, followed by only the necessary members of his team. Bella, his assistant, had pleaded to come along. At the last minute, he gave her the pith helmet and khaki uniform all who entered had to wear.

Klopfer ducked his head and stepped into the

darkness of the tomb. He paused and took a deep breath. Was the air he breathed really five thousand years old?

A smile crossed his face. In a few hours, he knew he would be the envy of scientists around the world.

Klopfer's boots scraped the tunnel floor, sending up a curtain of dust. The tunnel headed down. The air grew warmer with every step. The lights held by the team crisscrossed the walls and floor as they walked.

Klopfer took a deep breath, trying to calm himself, to slow his heartbeat. He could feel his hot sweat drench the back of his neck. "Unbearable excitement," he murmured to himself.

He raised his face to a video camera that was trained on him. "We are about to make history," he said. "We are about to uncover something the world has not seen in five thousand years."

He turned to Bella Wortham, who walked a few steps behind him. "I will need you to write the first report," he told her. "The first impressions. The first thoughts upon seeing Arragotus."

She smiled. "So I guess you're glad you decided to bring me along?"

Klopfer didn't reply. His mind was whirling with ideas of what was about to happen.

They finally reached the chamber where Arragotus rested in his stone case. It seemed to take forever to get the work crew in place.

Klopfer stopped a few feet away. Wortham stayed close at his side. Six workers lined up on each side of the mummy case.

Klopfer could barely breathe as they gripped the heavy lid and slowly began to slide it off the case. The lid made a whining, scraping sound that echoed down the long tunnel.

Video cameras were trained on the case. All eyes were on the lid as the workers struggled to move it away.

"Yes!" Klopfer let out a cry as the case was opened. "This is the moment, everyone! This is *history*!"

Heart thudding in his chest, he moved forward. His legs felt as if they weighed a thousand pounds each. His whole body trembled with excitement.

Holding his breath, Klopfer stepped up to the tall case. He leaned over and peered inside.

It was empty.

Dr. Klopfer let out a choking gasp. He gripped the side of the mummy case as his knees started to collapse. Two crew members hurried to prop him up and keep him from falling.

Startled cries echoed all around.

"Turn off the video recorders!" Klopfer cried in a shrill, trembling voice. "Turn them off. Now!"

He raised his eyes to see Bella. She was staring at the side of the coffin.

Still breathing hard, Klopfer began to feel a little stronger. "What are you gazing at?" he called to his assistant.

"Do you see this ancient writing?" she replied. "I can make out a few words. But I don't know what they mean."

Klopfer frowned. "Probably just a telling of the ridiculous curse."

"But maybe they reveal where the mummy of Arragotus is hiding?" Wortham said.

Klopfer backed up a few steps. Crew members

shone lights on the coffin's side. He scanned the strange words quickly.

"Yes, I can read it," he said. He squinted hard. "I can read it, but I can't make any sense of it."

Wortham stared at him. "What does it say?"

Klopfer read the words: "ABASEEGO MODARO LAMADOROS CREBEN!"

A hush fell over the chamber as the words rang over the walls and down the tunnel. Klopfer continued to stare at the strange inscription, as if hypnotized.

"Can you translate, Dr. Klopfer?" Wortham's voice stirred him from his thoughts.

"No," he said. "I told you. I have no idea what they mean. They don't appear to have any meaning at all. They—"

He stopped as a loud noise burst in front of him. A cracking sound. Like wood breaking.

He and Wortham looked down at the mummy case as another sound—a slow creaking—seemed to rise from inside.

The crew turned to the case. Video cameras began to record again.

Klopfer took a few steps closer to the side of the case—and gasped.

"The floor of the mummy case—it has cracked open!" he cried. He leaned over the side. "It has a false bottom. And the bottom is splitting. Something beneath it is—"

He never finished his sentence.

A hand shot up. An ugly hand swathed in bandages and tar. It burst through the bottom of the case.

It grabbed Klopfer's mustache—*and ripped it off his face.*

A chunk of skin came flying off with it.

Eyes bulging in horror, Klopfer opened his mouth in an animal howl of pain.

He started to slide to the floor. But before he collapsed, the false bottom cracked wide open, and the ancient mummy sat up. He grabbed Klopfer. Clawed at his face. Clawed until there was no face left.

Shrill screams and horrified cries bounced off the chamber walls.

Klopfer fell to the floor. He lay sprawled on his stomach beside the case. Blood dripped off the mummy's wrapped hands. He uttered a low growl that seemed to come from deep inside his belly.

The ancient hands gripped both sides of the case. With another groan, Arragotus struggled to pull himself up. Everyone could see he was about to climb out of his coffin.

"Somebody—do something!" a man screamed. "*Do* something!"

Crew members stampeded into the tunnel. A wild scramble. They left their equipment behind and ran screaming.

Bella Wortham had a desperate idea. She turned to the strange words on the side of the mummy case. She squinted hard, struggling to make them out. Then she shouted them in a frightened voice:

"ABASEEGO MODARO LAMADOROS CREBEN!"

She gasped as the mummy stopped moving. His hands slid away from the coffin sides. His body relaxed. He settled onto his back on the cracked coffin bottom, arms at his side.

He didn't move.

"Quick!" Wortham shouted to the men who were still in the tomb, frozen there by their fear. "Cover him! Cover him!"

The crew members appeared to shake themselves from their daze. They moved to the coffin lid and struggled to hoist the heavy stone slab off the cavern floor.

The mummy remained asleep. He didn't move.

Groaning from the weight of the lid, the men raised it and slid it over the coffin.

Silence.

The only sounds now were the heavy breathing of the crew.

Wortham wiped the cold sweat off her forehead with her neckerchief. She took long, slow breaths, trying to calm her racing heartbeats.

"What next?" she wondered.

Two weeks later, she was sitting in Dr. Klopfer's hospital room. He had survived three surgeries to repair his face. His head was completely bandaged.

Mr. Amari entered the room. He twirled his white hat in his hands. "We were just discussing where to send the mummy," Wortham told him. "Dr. Klopfer doesn't want it sent to his science lab, after all."

A groan escaped Klopfer's mouth. The sound was muffled by the bandages that covered his entire head.

Wortham couldn't help but think, *The poor doctor looks like a mummy himself.*

After another groan, Klopfer's voice came out stronger. "I don't care where you send this mummy. Send it to Mars, for all I care. But do not send it to my lab."

Amari's gaze went from one to the other. "I urged you not to disturb the tomb. Now, this is your burden. You are responsible for this mummy. Not us."

Klopfer's head turned to Wortham. "Get rid of it! But be careful. The mummy is dangerous. Do not send it anywhere it could hurt people."

He coughed. Another groan. And then he cried, "Arragotus must never be seen again!"

PART TWO

5

My name is Aaron Riggles and I'm twelve. Mom, Dad, and my sister, Kristina, were sitting at the dinner table when I walked in.

Dad was already complaining about Mom's meatloaf because he doesn't like meatloaf and he likes to complain. He works in a tire store, and people come in and complain about their tires all day long. So Dad has to get *his* complaining in when he gets home.

"Hey, check this out," I said. I have a scratchy voice that makes me sound like a frog with a cold. I hate it. And I hate the freckles all over my cheeks and my red hair.

But what can I do?

Kristina and I don't look like we're in the same family. Her hair is long and straight and black, and her skin is pale like Mom's. Actually, she looks like a Mom clone, and I don't look like anyone.

I came into the dining room dragging a long wooden chest behind me. It looked a little like a pirate's treasure chest.

"You're late," Dad grumbled.

"Tell me something I don't know," I replied. Dad says I have a "smart mouth," and Dad is right. Is that a bad thing?

"What are you dragging in here?" Mom asked, helping herself from the bowl of string beans. "Where did you get that?"

I mopped the sweat off my forehead with the sleeve of my T-shirt. "At school," I said.

They all stared at the wooden chest. The wood was scratched up and stained. The metal clasps were rusted. The chest appeared to be very old.

"A puppeteer came to school," I said, leaning on my chair at the table. "He called himself Mandrake the Great."

"Cornball name," Dad muttered. "Were his puppets as lame as his name?"

"No," I said. I love puppets. I have two clown marionettes up in my room that I play with a lot. I make them dance and bow to each other, and I do whole shows just for myself.

Kristina says that makes me a weirdo freak. But who asked her?

"Mandrake put on a funny assembly," I said. "He had about six puppets, and he did different voices for each one. It was a little babyish, but everyone liked it anyway."

Dad took a long drink of water. "You're not explaining about the chest."

"I'm getting to it," I said. "I was leaving school, and I saw Mandrake in the parking lot. He was loading his puppets into his SUV. So I went over and told him how I was into puppets, too. And I said I liked his show."

"You're still not explaining," Dad said.

"Give him a chance," Mom interrupted. She is always sticking up for me. Mom is the best.

"My meatloaf is getting cold," Dad complained. He always complains his food is too cold. Once, he complained that his ice cream was too cold. Seriously.

"I don't know why," I continued, "but Mandrake gave me this." I tapped my sneaker against the chest.

"It's one of his puppets?" Kristina asked.

"No," I said. "It's an old ventriloquist dummy. Mandrake said it was special. He said I could have it."

"Why?" Dad demanded. "Why did he give it to you?"

I shrugged. "He said he didn't need it anymore. He said he knew I'd give it a good home."

Kristina pushed her chair back and slid away from the table. "Let's see it! What does it look like?" she asked.

She bent down and knocked on the lid. "Anyone home?"

Two metal clasps held the lid down. I flipped one up, and Kristina flipped the other one.

Mom and Dad stood behind us. I slowly pulled the heavy lid open. We all gazed at the grinning dummy on its back, resting on a shiny red cloth inside the chest.

The dummy had a big wooden head with dark brown hair painted on the top. Big green eyes. The wood on his sharp nose had a small chip in it. His grinning mouth was painted bright red.

He was dressed in a wrinkled gray suit. His white shirt had a dark stain on the collar. His red bow tie was crooked. His brown leather shoes were scuffed.

"Mandrake said the dummy's name is Slappy," I said. "Look. There are a bunch of papers that come with him."

"Did you read the instructions?" Dad asked.

"Nope," I said.

Mom made a face. "He's very ugly," she said softly.

"You should know!" the dummy shouted.

24

We all laughed.

Dad squatted down to see the dummy closer. "It really does talk. That's genius."

"*Yes. Genius,*" the dummy said. "*Don't be jealous. Just because your IQ is the same number as your shoe size!*"

We laughed again.

"Awesome," Kristina said.

"Maybe he has voice recognition software?" I said.

"What does that mean?" Dad asked. "He can hear you when you talk to him?"

"No," I said. "It means you can talk to him, and he will talk back to you."

"He's programmed to say things?" Kristina asked. "Cool. Take him out of the case, Aaron. Can I hold him?"

The dummy appeared to stare right at her. "*Don't hold me,*" he said. "*Hold your breath. It stinks!*"

I laughed.

"I don't know if I like this dummy," Mom said. "He's very nasty, Aaron."

"*Talk about* nasty," Slappy said. "*Have you smelled your dinner?*"

"Maybe you should leave him in the case," Mom said to me.

"Don't worry, Mom," I said. "Mandrake gave me his phone number. See?" I pulled the small slip of paper from my jeans pocket. "He said if there's a problem, I can call anytime. He said he'll come and take the dummy back."

Slappy appeared to gaze at me. "*Is that really your face?*" he rasped. "*Or did a bird fly over and drop something on your neck?*"

I couldn't help it. That joke made me laugh. But I was the only one who did. Mom and Dad and Kristina stared at the grinning dummy in silence.

"I'm sorry," Mom said, shaking her head. "But I think he is a little creepy."

I lifted Slappy from the chest. "Mom, listen," I said. "He just has a bunch of jokes programmed into him. It's NOT like he's alive . . ."

I propped the dummy up in the empty chair next to my seat. Mom cut a slice of meatloaf for me and placed a baked potato beside it on my plate.

Dad scooted behind me on his way to the kitchen.

"Where are you going?" Mom asked.

"To get ketchup for my meatloaf," he said.

Mom shook her head. "It hurts my feelings when you drown your meatloaf in ketchup."

"But I like ketchup," Dad replied. He disappeared into the kitchen.

I took a few bites of meatloaf. Then I turned to the dummy. "Slappy, would you like to eat dinner with us?"

The dummy's wooden lips clicked up and down. *"I'd rather throw up my intestines!"* he growled.

"Ooh, that's *horrible!*" Mom cried.

"Not as horrible as that big wart on your neck!" the dummy cried. *"Or is that your* head?"

Dad returned carrying the ketchup bottle.

"Aaron, I think you'd better take Slappy away from the table."

Mom nodded. "Yes, definitely. Whoever programmed those awful jokes is totally twisted." She turned to my sister. "Kristina, don't you agree?"

She hesitated. "Well . . . it's kind of funny," she said. "Kind of."

"I think he's a riot," I said.

"Please take him away," Mom said. "He's spoiling our dinner."

"*The only thing that's spoiled is the* meat!" Slappy rasped. "*You better line up at the bathroom* now!"

"That's going too far!" Mom cried, tossing her fork to the table.

Dad's meatloaf was buried under an avalanche of ketchup. He squinted at the dummy. "So weird. It really does seem to listen to what you say."

Dad was right. This programming was awesome.

"Please take it away," Mom repeated.

"Let's give him one more chance," I said. I turned the dummy so that it was facing me. "Slappy, you're going to be a good boy, aren't you?"

"*Say that again,*" Slappy replied, "*and I'll eat your heart like a meatball.*"

"That's enough," Dad said, jumping to his feet. He had a big ketchup stain on his shirt. You can

28

always tell what Dad had for dinner by reading his shirt.

Dad moved around the table and grabbed Slappy by the neck. "I'm taking him in the other room, Aaron," Dad said. "I think there's a problem with the voice programming. Someone gave him a bad personality."

"*Before I go,*" Slappy spoke up, "*I just want to offer my sincere thanks for the meal.*"

Startled, Dad let go of the dummy and took a step back.

Slappy leaned forward over the table. Then he opened his mouth wide, tilted back his head— and began to spew wave after wave of a thick green liquid into the air.

Splurrrp splurrrrp splurrrrrp!

"Ohhhh." A groan escaped my throat. The smell was *sickening*!

The green gunk splashed over our dinner table, rolled over the food bowls, covered our plates.

The dummy made disgusting, gross vomit sounds deep in his throat as he spewed the green gunk over all of us. I tried to duck away, and I felt a hot wave of goo sweep over my head and cover my hair.

Dad had been standing right behind the dummy. But he was so startled and grossed out, he froze for a long moment. Finally, he spun the dummy into the air, lifting it out of the chair.

The dummy splashed the disgusting green goo over Dad's face and down the front of his shirt. I felt sick. The smell was overwhelming. I tried to hold my breath, but I couldn't get the odor out of my nose and mouth.

Dad shook the dummy hard. He turned it away from him and fumbled for the controls under the dummy's jacket. Then he turned it over and ran his hand under the dummy's white shirt.

"I can't turn it off!" Dad cried. "Shouldn't there be a way to shut him off? How do you do it?"

Slappy let out one last *urrrrp*. He stopped spewing. His eyes closed. His grin appeared to grow wider.

"Oh, thank goodness!" I cried. My T-shirt and jeans were drenched. My hair was sticky and matted to my head with the goo.

"How are we going to clean this mess?" Kristina cried.

Dad's face was bright red with anger. He was breathing hard. He gripped the dummy around the waist.

"*Pardon my manners*," Slappy said. Then he tossed back his head and giggled.

Mom wiped the sticky goo off her hands on the sides of her dress. She gave me a gentle push. "Quick. Call the number. Tell that puppet guy to come get his dummy as fast as he can."

The sheet of paper trembled in my hand. I

tugged my phone from my pocket. I had to wipe a glob of green gunk off the phone.

My hand shook so much, I had to punch in the number three times. My thumb kept slipping off the screen.

I held my breath, trying to make the smell go away. I knew I'd be smelling it for weeks!

"Tell that guy to hurry over here!" Kristina cried.

The phone rang once. Twice.

A man's voice came on. "Friendly Hardware. Simon speaking."

I hesitated. "Uh . . . is Mandrake there?"

"Who?"

"Mandrake? Mandrake the puppeteer?"

The man named Simon snickered. "There's no one named Mandrake here, son. This is a hardware store. Not a puppet show."

I nearly dropped the phone. "Are you sure?"

Simon snickered again. "Of course I'm sure."

"S-sorry," I stammered. I hung up. I lowered the phone to my side and turned to my family. "Mandrake gave me a wrong number. We can't return Slappy."

Mom scowled and shook her head. "That wasn't an accident," she muttered. "He didn't want you to return this . . . monster."

Slappy tilted back his head and laughed. *"Would one of you wipe the goo off my chin? I got a little on me."*

"What are we going to *do*?" Kristina cried. "This is sick. Totally sick. The green vomit—it's everywhere. I—I—" My sister was so upset, I thought she was about to cry.

Slappy turned his wooden head to face me. *"Can I help it if I had an upset tummy? Hahaha."*

"But—why—?" I choked out.

"I just wanted to make sure you're all paying attention," he rasped. *"Life is going to be fine around here—unless you disobey my orders."*

"Orders?" I cried. "You want us to take orders from *you*?"

"Enough!" Dad shouted. He swung the dummy

around and lowered it into the wooden chest. "Enough!"

The dummy started to sit up, but Dad slammed the heavy lid down hard. Then he squatted and carefully snapped both metal latches.

"I know just what to do with him," Dad said, dragging the chest out of the room.

"But, Dad—" I started.

Dad raised a hand to silence me. "You three stay and get started on the cleanup. I'll be back in a short while."

"And don't worry," he said as he headed out the door. "You'll never see Slappy in *this* house again."

PART THREE

9

Cathy O'Connor. That's me. Yes, I'm Colin O'Connor's daughter.

In Timberland Mills, just about everyone knows my dad. That's because he owns the Haunted Horror Museum on Shadow Street.

It's the only museum here, and schools start taking classes there for field trips in first or second grade. I mean, there isn't much else you'd want to visit in our small town.

I'm twelve, and my class is having an overnight at the museum next Friday night. Some kids are excited and a few are a little freaked to spend the night with a real mummy, and a dinosaur skull and some bones, and insect fossils, and mummified snakes and reptiles.

But to be perfectly honest, I think the museum is kind of lame. I guess it's because I grew up inside it. I spent time examining all the old fossils and dinosaur bones and the vampire bats and my dad's fake werewolf when I was five years old. That stuff doesn't exactly give me shivers anymore.

My sister, Shannon, is nine and gets excited about things a lot more than I do. But she is like me. She's kind of "been there, done that."

The only thing that's sort of exciting is that Dad finally got a real mummy for the museum. Dad has been trying to get his hands on an ancient mummy for years. He put out ads all over the Internet for private collectors and archaeologists. And then one day, someone answered all the way from Egypt. We got our mummy!

The museum is so tiny and our town is so small. Who would guess that Dad's plan would work?

Believe me, that mummy will get a lot of attention at our class overnight. A lot of kids are into horror movies and scary books.

But to tell the truth, I don't get it. Those things are mostly just gross, aren't they? And what's the fun of grossing yourself out or giving yourself shivers?

I know we hurt Dad's feelings when we make jokes about his museum and make fun of his scary stuff. But he loves scaring people so much . . . the whole thing gets him so *psyched* . . . I guess Shannon and I think it's our job to bring him back to earth.

Even though Shannon and I are three years apart, we're very close. We look like sisters. We both have straight black hair and dark brown eyes. We both have kind of round faces, baby faces (yuck), that make us look younger than we are.

We get along really well most of the time. We don't fight like a lot of sisters do. I have only one main problem with my sister.

She's a mad tickler.

She's always tickling me and my friends, and she thinks it's a riot. Even when we beg her to stop.

Our cousin Logan is in my class. And sometimes when he comes over, I have to tackle Shannon and wrestle her off him to get her to stop tickling him.

Poor Logan *hates* to be tickled. It actually gives him hiccups. Guess what? Shannon says that's why she likes to tickle him.

The worst part about Shannon's tickling obsession is that her hands are always cold. Don't ask me why. But it feels like your skin is being attacked by ice cubes.

Anyway, on Thursday night, Shannon, Logan, and I were in the Haunted Horror Museum after dinner. (It's not really haunted. Dad just wishes it was.)

We were supposed to be helping Dad set everything up for the class overnight. Shannon had been tickling Logan in the backseat of our SUV, and now he had the hiccups. Dad started to pull cots into the dinosaur room. He motioned for us to get to work.

But Logan, squeaking with hiccups, decided to

pay Shannon back for the tickling attack. He picked up a ball from the top of a display case and heaved it at her. "Think fast!" he shouted.

Shannon caught the ball in one hand and made a disgusted face. "Hey, it's sticky."

"Please put that down," Dad called from across the room. "That's not a ball. That's a whale eyeball."

"Oops," Logan said.

I laughed. Shannon looked a little sick. She set the eyeball down on a tabletop. She wiped her hands on the sides of her sweatshirt.

"Hey, is Shannon coming tomorrow night, too?" I called to Dad.

"Yes, she is. She's my assistant," Dad said. "I need her here tomorrow night." Dad started to drag another cot across the hall. "She promises she won't tickle anyone—*don't* you, Shannon?"

Shannon grinned and didn't reply.

"The boys in your class are lucky. They'll get to sleep in the mummy room with our brand-new mummy," Dad said. "We'll put the girls in the dinosaur room."

"No one will be able to sleep," I said. "They'll be shaking and shivering too hard."

Logan laughed. "Most kids will be so scared, they'll probably cry themselves to sleep!" The museum didn't scare Logan either.

Shannon and I laughed along with Logan.

"You're not funny," Dad muttered. "I'm so tired

of your sarcasm. Aren't you the least bit excited that we finally have a mummy here? You know I've been wanting a real mummy ever since I opened the museum."

"That was a win," I said. "Sorry about our bad attitude. We're just snobs, I guess."

Now Dad was laughing. "I know you think this place isn't scary. But wouldn't you be surprised if something totally frightening happened here in the museum tomorrow night?"

"Totally," Logan and I said in unison.

10

We helped Dad line up the cots in both rooms. Then we headed to the little snack bar in the basement. We climbed onto tall stools and served ourselves chips and drinks.

Shannon reached a hand out and tried to tickle Logan's chin. But he ducked away, and she almost fell off her stool.

Dad appeared, mopping sweat off his forehead with a handkerchief. It was hot and stuffy in the museum, but he couldn't afford air conditioning.

"Follow me," he said. "I want to show you something. You've probably seen it before, but it's pretty awesome."

We followed him up the front staircase. He took us to the end of the hall, into his office. He slid out a desk drawer. He picked up a handful of shiny little stones. I took one from his hand.

It wasn't a stone. It appeared to be darkened glass. I squinted hard into it and saw a large winged insect. "Dad, you never showed us these."

He smiled. "See? I still have a few surprises."

Logan held one up to the light. "There's a bug inside. How did it get there?"

"These are thousands and thousands of years old," Dad said. "The insects got trapped in tree resin and then became fossils."

"Trapped inside these stones?" I asked, spinning mine in my hand.

"Resin is a liquid that drips down the trunks of trees," Dad explained. "The insects got caught in it thousands of years ago. Then the resin hardened into these amber stones. And preserved them perfectly."

"They look like they could be alive," Logan said.

"Creepy," Shannon murmured. She handed hers back to Dad.

Dad raised a couple of them to the light. "Mean-looking bugs," he said. "Look at the sharp pincers on this one."

"What are you going to do with them?" I asked.

Dad clicked the two oval pieces of amber together. "I have over a hundred of them," he said. "Shannon and I are going to hide them around the museum. We can have a scavenger hunt for them tomorrow night."

I rolled my eyes. "A scavenger hunt? Like our birthday parties when we were six?"

Dad dropped the pieces of amber into the drawer and slid it shut. "Give me a break, Cathy.

These fossils are rare and very valuable. I think everyone will be excited to hunt for them."

"Our class?" Logan chimed in. "Our class will be excited to hunt for slices of pizza."

I laughed.

Dad scowled at me. "We'll have pizza, too," he muttered. "But since we are here in a horror museum, I think we should use what we have to entertain everyone. I don't think kids will find ancient insect fossils or a mummy boring or babyish. I—"

He stopped because the doorbell rang. The bell to the back door. It clanged loudly once . . . twice . . . three times.

Dad turned and started toward the stairs. "Who could be here this time of night?" he asked. "Who would come to the back door?"

We followed him down the stairs. He turned the locks on the door and slid the latch open. Then he pushed the door open, and we heard him cry out, "How weird!"

11

I saw him bent over, struggling with something on the ground. "Dad, can I help?" I started to the door.

But he turned and stepped inside. He pulled a long wooden chest into the building. "How strange is this?" he said breathlessly.

He set it down in the middle of the hall and took a few seconds to catch his breath. "I saw a car speed away when I opened the door," he said. "Then I looked down and saw this chest."

Logan took a step back. "Do you hear anything inside? Is there an animal in there?"

We all listened. Silence.

"Only one way to find out what our mystery box holds," Dad said.

We gathered around as he leaned over and snapped the two rusted latches on the front of the chest. Then he put both hands on the lid and shoved it open.

I gasped. We all stared at a large ventriloquist

dummy. He lay on his back in a wrinkled gray suit, a white shirt, and a crooked red bow tie. He appeared to stare up at us with glassy green eyes.

"Totally weird," I muttered.

"He's way ugly," Logan said. "Look at that sick grin on his face."

"His nose has a big chip at the end," Shannon pointed out. "The dummy looks pretty old."

Dad scratched the top of his head. "Guess someone wanted to donate it to the museum. But why did they do it at night? And why did they hurry away like that?"

Shannon reached for it. "Can I try it? Can I make it talk?"

"Not now," Dad said. "I think—" He stopped. He was staring at a bunch of rolled-up papers tucked at the dummy's side. "What are these?"

He tugged them out and unrolled them. He scanned the first page quickly. "Hmmmm . . . Says the dummy *is* very old. His name is Slappy. Slappy seems to have a long history."

I felt a shiver run down my body. I had the crazy feeling the dummy was staring at *me*. Just a wild thought, but it gave me a sudden tingle of fear.

Dad rolled up the papers and stuffed them back into the case. "I'll have to read all the info later," he said. "I think I have the perfect empty display case for this dummy."

46

He shut the lid and slid the chest against the wall. "Still a lot of decorating to do," he said.

"Yeah. Where are the plastic bats?" I asked. "We can start hanging them around."

"I think I stacked them in my office," Dad said. He glanced at his watch. "Oh, wow. I promised to pick your mother up. She's working late tonight. I've got to run."

He began to hurry toward the front entrance. "I'll be back in twenty minutes. Hang up the bats and blow up the black balloons. The helium tank is outside the mummy room. I'll get back as fast as I can."

The door banged shut behind him.

Shannon turned to me. "Cathy, did Dad seem a little frantic to you just now?"

I laughed. "When isn't he frantic? The overnight means a lot to him. He loves having kids stay at the museum. He looks forward to it every year. Let's get to work," I said. "Shannon, come with me. We'll put up the bat decorations. Logan, why don't you start on the balloons?"

He gave me a quick two-fingered salute. "Aye, aye, Captain."

We split up. Logan headed toward the mummy room at the end of the hall. Shannon led the way upstairs to the office.

It took us a while to find the black plastic bats. Dad had them buried beneath a big stack of papers. Dad isn't the most organized person in the world. Actually, he's a total slob. Seriously. The big trash dumpster behind the museum is neater than Dad's office.

Shannon and I worked together, hanging the bats on the walls. We put a few in the mummy room, where the boys would be sleeping.

Deep in its case, the mummy appeared to gaze at the ceiling as we worked. I thought about leaving a bat on its chest, but that seemed kind of lame.

The mummy was creepy. It didn't need any decoration.

The mummy was the newest display in the building, and Dad couldn't talk about anything else. He said it made his horror museum complete.

A real mummy—thousands of years old. Dad has spent so much time lately reading up on it. He has stacks of paper on his desk about the letters and symbols on the mummy case. The whole first week it was here he did etchings and charcoal rubbings of the ancient words, trying to figure out what they meant.

How weird to think that someone's all-time dream was a mummy. But . . . that's my dad.

After we finished in the mummy room, my sister and I headed to the front, on our way to the dinosaur bones room.

"Hey—!" Shannon grabbed my arm and pulled me to a stop.

I turned to where she was looking—and gasped.

What's up with this?

The dummy was sitting on top of his chest with his legs dangling to the floor.

"What are you staring at?" he rasped. *"Get back to work!"*

12

A "gawwwwllllp" sound escaped my open mouth. Shannon squeezed my arm harder.

Then Logan's grinning face popped up from behind the chest. He shook his head. "You are too easy to scare. You should have seen your faces!"

"We weren't scared," I said. "We were just surprised."

"*Don't try to fool a dummy!*" Logan said in a tinny voice, working the dummy's mouth.

I brushed Shannon's hand away and strode up to Logan. "Why are you playing with that? Why aren't you blowing up balloons?"

"I couldn't get the helium tank to work," he said. "I think the valve is stuck. So I decided to give you two a thrill."

"Can I hold Slappy?" Shannon didn't wait for Logan to answer. She lifted the dummy off the chest. "Whoa." She almost dropped him. Slappy was nearly as tall as Shannon!

Shannon sat on the chest and arranged the dummy on her lap. Its big wooden head toppled over and hit her on the shoulder. "How do you work his mouth?" she asked Logan.

"How do you work YOUR mouth?" the dummy rasped.

"Stop it, Logan," Shannon said. "Answer my question."

Logan raised both hands in the air. "I didn't make it say that. It wasn't me."

"Shut up, Logan," I said. "You're not going to scare us again."

"Seriously, Cathy. I didn't say that."

"How do you work the mouth?" Shannon repeated. "Tell me."

"You put your hand in its back," Logan told her.

Shannon fumbled under the dummy's sports jacket.

"Stop it! I'm ticklish!" Slappy cried.

Shannon jerked her hand away.

"It wasn't me!" Logan said, shaking his head. "You've got to believe me. I didn't say that. This is too weird."

Shannon stood up and propped the dummy against the wall. "There's something weird going on here," she said. "Maybe the dummy is programmed to say stuff."

I pushed open the lid to the chest and lifted the stack of papers out. They were old and yellow, crinkled up with tiny type on them.

I raised the first page and read through it quickly.

"What does it say?" Shannon asked. "Does it give instructions?"

I read a little more, squinting at the tiny type. "No. No instructions," I said.

I turned to the second page, reading quickly. "It says the dummy was made more than a hundred years ago. Whoa . . . By an evil magician. It says . . . Wait . . . It says Slappy has powers."

All three of us turned to stare at the dummy.

"Powers?" Logan said.

"It says the dummy has an evil curse on it," I continued. "It brings evil wherever it goes."

Shannon laughed. "Dad will *love* that!" she exclaimed.

"Perfect for this museum," I said.

"Someone had fun making this up," Logan said. "You don't believe it—do you?"

"Of course not," I said.

"Dad probably will," Shannon said.

I uttered a short cry. "Did that dummy just blink?"

Logan made a face. "Now *you're* trying to scare *us*? Get real."

"I thought I saw it blink. Really." I raised the papers to my face and read some more. "There are a bunch of strange words here," I said. "I don't know what language they're in."

"Probably dummy language," Logan said.

Shannon turned to him. "You speak Dummy, don't you, Logan?" She tried to tickle his chin, but he backed away.

"Quiet," I said. "This is interesting. It says if we read the words out loud, Slappy will come to life."

Shannon and Logan laughed. "Someone has seen too many horror movies," Logan said.

"Have you seen your face?" The dummy lifted his head. *"You belong in a horror movie!"*

I gasped. This was way too creepy. How did he know what we were saying?

I walked up beside Slappy and tapped the top of his head with my fist. "Who's in there?"

"My brain *is in there!"* the dummy rasped. *"Something I'm sure you've never heard of! Hahaha!"*

All three of us took a step back. "Someone programmed him to say those things," Shannon said.

"I'll program YOU!" the dummy shouted. *"I'll teach you how to wave bye-bye! Your parents will be so impressed! Haha!"*

Logan turned pale. "This isn't funny," he murmured. "It's like he can hear us."

"I can see *you, too!"* the dummy exclaimed. *"Wish I could* unsee *you! I'll have nightmares tonight."*

"It . . . it's alive!" I stammered.

"I wish Dad was here," Shannon said, backing away.

"*Was that your dad?*" Slappy rasped. "*I thought a buffalo escaped from the zoo!*"

"This . . . this is too scary," Logan said. "Let's shut him back up in the case."

"*I'll shut you up!*" the dummy cried. "*I'll be giving the orders from now on!*"

"Grab him!" I said. "He . . . he's dangerous. We have to lock him back up."

Logan and I dove for him. But to our surprise, the dummy could run—and run fast! As he took off, Shannon grabbed one arm. But Slappy tugged hard, almost pulling her off her feet.

As he sped down the hall, he tossed back his head and let out a long, ugly laugh that echoed off the walls.

My heart pounded as I chased after him, Logan and Shannon close behind. "Whoa! Look—!" I cried as Slappy suddenly turned and ran through an open door.

Dad's office.

What did he want in there?

Gasping for breath, I stepped into the doorway. And saw the dummy sweep a hand over Dad's desk. He sent a tall stack of papers flying to the floor. He grabbed a glass paperweight and smashed it on the wall.

I moved to grab him with my free hand. I was still gripping the papers from the dummy's box in the other one.

Slappy laughed that ugly laugh again. "*Looks*

like you're in trouble!" he rasped. *"Dad's office is a mess—and he won't blame ME! Hahaha."*

Logan and Shannon tried to squeeze past me. But Logan bumped me from behind. Slappy's papers fell from my hand. I scrambled to pick them up.

Shannon and Logan grabbed the dummy around the waist. Logan pinned Slappy's hands behind his back so he couldn't do any more damage.

My hand was trembling as I tried to pick up the scattered papers. Actually, my whole body was trembling.

I couldn't believe this was happening. It was too crazy . . . too terrifying.

I don't know why, but I raised the paper to my face. I didn't really think about it. The words on the page—the strange words that were supposed to bring the dummy to life—shook before my eyes.

I squinted hard at them. And without thinking, I said them out loud:

"KARRU MARRI ODONNA LOMA MOLONU KARRANO."

13

I lowered the paper and stared at the dummy. Shannon and Logan walked closer to it.

"Whoa. Look," I whispered.

The dummy's eyes closed. Its head tilted to one side. Its mouth dropped open and stayed open. It didn't move.

Shannon laughed. "We didn't bring it to life. We put it to sleep!"

I heard a sound. A footstep?

"Where are you?" a familiar voice shouted. Dad's voice.

He trotted over to us. "Why is this place such a mess? What are you doing in my office? You were supposed to be decorating, not making a mess! Did you hang the bats? Blow up the balloons?"

We all started talking at once.

"The dummy—he's alive!"

"It was totally creepy! The dummy talked to us!"

"He made fun of us. He has a cruel sense of humor. He's totally mean."

Dad grinned and shook his head. "Don't kid a kidder. *I'm* the one who plays the jokes around here."

"You've got to believe us. He's alive, Dad. We're serious. He's alive—and he's scary."

"You're going to have to try harder than that," Dad laughed.

We argued with him. We pleaded for him to believe us.

He walked over to the dummy and held him up. "Hello, Slappy," he said. "Can you talk?"

The dummy's head slumped down. He was silent.

Dad shook him. "Talk to me, Slappy. Are you alive? Or are they pulling my leg?"

The dummy bounced lifelessly in Dad's hands.

Dad raised his eyes to us. "You call this *alive*? Can we finish up what we have to do and go home? I'll straighten my office tomorrow.

"Take him," Dad said, handing the dummy to Logan. "Take him upstairs. I'll lock him in a display case."

"No. Please, Dad—" I said. "You've got to get rid of him. He's dangerous."

"We'll be careful with him," Dad insisted. He grinned. "Just in case he comes to life again."

Dad didn't believe us.

Logan took Slappy from Dad and pushed it into the wooden chest. He carried it upstairs.

"Let's go," Dad said when Logan returned.

57

"Mom needs help with dinner, so we better get back home."

My legs were trembling as I followed Dad to the car. Chills rolled down my back.

A dummy that comes to life? And hurts people?

I was scared. I was seriously scared.

But . . . the fact is, I was afraid *too soon.*

The true horror didn't begin until one hour before the overnight began.

SLAPPY HERE, EVERYONE.

Do you know what the baby mummy said when he got lost in the woods? "I miss my mummy!"

What did the mummy say when he wanted to quit work and go home? "Hey, guys, let's wrap it up!"

Hahaha. I love mummy jokes, don't you?

But I have the feeling this new mummy in the horror museum is no joke.

I mean, it's GOT to be Arragotus—right? The museum's the perfect place for that bag of Kleenex.

Tell me, what kind of name is Arragotus?

It sounds like someone barfing up his lunch! Hahaha.

Do you think Arragotus will come to life?

He'd better. If he doesn't, this will be a very short story!

Hahaha.

14

Friday night Dad was running through the schedule with Logan and me. "When the kids arrive, everyone can put their bags down on their cots. And then we'll meet here in the main hall," he said.

Dad had to spend most of the day getting his office back in order. What order, I don't know. It was always a mess. This was just a different kind of mess than he was used to. But he seemed happy and excited.

He loves having school classes stay overnight in his museum. It gives him a chance to show off his big collections. And he likes giving kids a few scares.

Logan and I were pretty excited, too. How awesome to party all night with our friends.

Stacks of boxes with pizza had arrived. Black balloons floated overhead. The bat decorations covered the walls. And Dad had tested the museum sound system so we could crank up the music.

"We can start in the mummy room," Dad said. "I know everyone will want to see the new mummy as soon as they arrive. Good old Arragotus. He is going to be a star."

"Arragotus?" I said. "Is that the mummy's name?"

Dad nodded. "I've been doing a lot of research about him, but he's still quite a mystery."

"That mummy is totally creepy," Logan said. "The kids are going to freak when they see him."

"I guess the dinosaur is the second stop," Dad continued. "I know parts are missing. But we have the head and the torso and three legs." He smiled at me. "Someday we'll have a *whole* dinosaur. That will be awesome."

"Awesome," I repeated. I liked seeing Dad in such a good mood.

Glancing at a small notepad, Dad continued telling us the schedule. "After the dinosaur, we can have the scavenger hunt for the petrified insects in amber."

"What about the pizza?" Logan smiled.

"We can eat after the scavenger hunt," Dad said. He closed his notepad and shoved it into his pocket.

"You're not going to show off that new dummy, right?" Logan asked.

"Not yet, Logan. There will be plenty of other things to scare the kids," Dad said. "He's locked in a glass case where nobody can mess with him.

I want to take a better look at him before I introduce him to an audience."

A noise from down the hall made him stop. It sounded like a deep groan. A human groan.

We all turned and gazed down the long hall.

I heard it again. Louder this time.

And then a girl's shrill scream—a scream of horror.

I let out a cry. Dad gasped. "Where's Shannon?"

I gazed all around. "I thought she was here. I didn't realize—"

Another scream rang off the walls.

"Shannon? Shannon?" Dad cried. He took off running. Logan and I followed.

To the mummy room. At the doorway, Dad stopped short. Logan and I almost bumped right into him.

The room was bathed in blue light. The dark walls glowed eerily, reflecting the light. A large model of a pyramid also shone brightly in the glow.

Shannon stood with her back pressed against the wall. Her eyes were wide with fear. "I—I—I—" she sputtered.

"Shannon—what's wrong?" I screamed.

She pointed with a trembling finger to the mummy case. "I—I said some words. They were on the side of the mummy case. I said them and—"

Another low groan made us turn.

"Oh no," Dad murmured. His eyes bulged.

I opened my mouth to scream, but no sound came out.

I grabbed Logan's arm as we stared . . . stared at the mummy sitting up in his case.

15

The mummy's wrapped hands gripped the sides of the stone case. His head tilted forward. His chest leaned forward and another ugly low groan came from somewhere deep inside him.

"Oh noooo," Dad moaned again.

"He . . . he's *moving*!" Logan cried.

Shannon slid up beside Dad and wrapped her arms around his waist. "I just wanted to see it," she said. "I just wanted to take a peek. Then I saw the words on the coffin, and I said them. I didn't mean to—"

Dad gently pushed her back. "Get out," he said, his voice tense. "Get out of the room."

I choked. My mouth was suddenly dry. Chill after chill ran down my back.

"Those words brought him to life," I choked out. "Just like the dummy."

We stood frozen, watching in shock as the mummy pressed both hands down on the sides of the case, his ancient arms crackling and cracking from the pressure.

He turned and stopped, as if seeing us for the first time. Then, with another groan, he raised one leg over the case.

"He—he's climbing out," I stammered. "Dad—what are you going to do?"

Dad's face was tomato red. He had big drops of sweat rolling down his forehead. "I don't know," he murmured. "My brain isn't functioning. This . . . this can't be real."

The mummy stood outside the case now. He rolled his head from side to side. From beneath the ancient layers of cloth and tar, we heard more cracking sounds. Like bones breaking.

Arragotus took a heavy step toward us. He moved unsteadily in slow motion, testing his legs, his balance. He swayed to one side as he took another step.

"Should we call 911?" Shannon cried.

Dad shook his head. "They won't believe us. Who would believe this?"

The mummy raised his arms as he staggered toward us. As if he wanted to grab us . . . capture us . . . smother us.

"Maybe . . . maybe he's friendly," I said, my voice dry and tiny.

A growl rose up from deep in his chest.

"Not friendly," Logan said.

"Get back!" Dad shouted. He mopped sweat off his forehead with his hand. "Get back! I'm going to try—"

The mummy tossed his head to the side and howled, a throaty cry that echoed off the dark museum walls.

"I'm going to try to get him to return to his case," Dad said.

"How?" I cried.

"I don't know. Just don't get close," he ordered.

Logan, Shannon, and I stumbled to the wall. I bumped into an old iron battle shield and sent it clattering to the floor at my feet. Logan grabbed me to keep me from falling over it.

My heart pounding, I turned and watched Dad as he stepped toward the mummy. Dad raised a hand as if signaling the mummy to stop.

"Go back!" Dad cried. "Arragotus—go back to your bed. Go back to sleep!"

The mummy took another heavy step toward Dad. His wrapped feet thudded hard on the stone floor. His eyes were covered by a thick layer of tar. I knew he couldn't see.

But why did he appear to have his gaze locked on Dad?

"Go back!" Dad shouted again. He motioned with both hands. "Go back where you belong, Arragotus!"

The mummy had been moving slowly, an inch at a time. Testing his legs, unsure of his balance.

But now he lurched forward—and grabbed Dad by the neck.

Dad uttered a strangled cry. His hands flew up in surprise.

I screamed as the mummy hoisted Dad off the floor.

"Put him down! Let *go* of him!" I screamed.

Dad struggled to twist free of the mummy's grasp. But Arragotus was too strong. With a loud groan from deep in his chest, the mummy raised Dad high over his head . . .

. . . and heaved him facedown into the mummy case.

Dad hit hard. He made a sick *thud* as his body spread over the coffin bottom. Then he didn't move.

16

"Dad! Dad! Dad!" I couldn't stop. I kept scream-ing the word over and over.

Behind me, Logan and Shannon stood frozen in panic. Their eyes bulged in horror.

"Dad—move! Get out of there!" I cried.

The mummy turned. He bent over the case, as if examining Dad.

"Dad—please move! Please!" My cries echoed through all the rooms. "Dad—*please*!"

But he didn't move. He must have been knocked out when his head hit the stone bottom.

I sucked in a deep breath. My throat hurt from screaming.

The mummy reached his hands into the case. He took Dad by the shoulders and began to shake him.

"Cathy! Cathy! He's . . . he's going to *kill* him!" Shannon cried.

"No. No," I murmured. I hurtled across the room. I grabbed the mummy around the waist. The cloth-and-tar covering felt rough and hard on my skin. A sour odor, the odor of thousands of years, invaded my nose and mouth.

Dad's head bobbed lifelessly as the mummy continued to shake him by the shoulders. I tugged with all my strength, struggled to pull Arragotus away from Dad.

But the mummy was as solid as a tree trunk. I couldn't budge him.

"Get *off*!" I cried. "Let him go!" My voice was a harsh, terrified whisper.

The mummy whipped around suddenly, catching me off-balance. He swung his arm hard—and gave me a shove that sent me staggering back. I toppled to the floor. Waves of pain rolled up my whole body.

I saw the mummy turn again and reach down to grab Dad by the throat.

With a groan, I spun off the floor. Frantic, my mind spinning, red lights flashing in my eyes, I grabbed the armored shield I had knocked to the floor.

I lifted it in front of me—and raced to the mummy. I bashed the heavy metal shield into the mummy's side. The shield *clang*ed as it crashed into the mummy's hardened body.

Arragotus moaned and fell aside.

Gasping for breath, I watched him hit the floor. I heard rib bones cracking.

Inside the case, Dad blinked and raised his head.

"Dad—hurry. Get out!" I cried.

I grabbed Dad's arm to help him up. He kept blinking, tilting his head dizzily. Finally, he pulled himself over the side of the case. Rubbing the back of his neck, he leaned against the wall.

Struggling to catch my breath, I turned and saw the mummy climb to his feet. He took a slow step forward.

His arms reached out.

He glanced down at the shield.

He grunted and pointed at me. He kept his finger pointed, as if saying, *You're next!*

"Run, Cathy!" Shannon cried. "He's coming after *you* now."

I had been watching Dad, waiting for him to return to normal. But now I spun away. I started to the door.

Too late.

I felt the hard hands grip my shoulders. Hard as steel. The fingers dug into my skin.

I let out a cry of pain.

I squirmed and twisted. The mummy held on.

"Let me go!" I screamed.

Then, from somewhere deep in his throat, I heard a harsh whisper, a word, more a groan than a word. *"Cathy . . . Cathy . . ."*

"He can talk—and he knows your name!" Shannon screamed.

The mummy gripped me tighter.

"Cathy . . . Cathy . . ."

"Nooooo!" The sound of my name erupting

from his ancient throat sent chill after chill down my back—until my entire body shook. I couldn't breathe. I wanted to scream and scream and scream.

"Let me go! Let me go!"

"*Cathy . . .*"

The mummy raised his dry, scratchy hands to my neck. I felt the fingers begin to tighten.

"Nooo!" I screamed.

I raised my knee fast. Slammed it into the mummy's middle.

His hands loosened. It gave me just enough time to slip out of his grasp. I ducked fast and twirled away. I could still feel the dry, ancient hands on my throat.

I saw Dad try to take a step away from the wall. His eyes were still rolling in his head.

My breath came out in frantic whooshes. I struggled to think straight.

Suddenly, I had a plan.

My eyes on the mummy, I backed slowly toward the empty case. Arragotus grunted and started to follow me. "*Cathy . . . Cathy . . .*" He raised his hands again, preparing to attack, to grab me.

I backed up another step. Another.

I was nearly to the side of the mummy case.

Arragotus staggered forward slowly, steadily. His wrapped feet scraped the stone floor. One heavy *thump* . . . Another heavy *thump* . . .

"*Cathy* . . ." My name coming out of him in a disgusting rattle.

I waited till he was almost close enough to grab me. Then I ducked fast, spun away. Darted across the floor.

Summoning all my strength, I lifted the big model of the pyramid in both hands. I gripped it tightly and raised it in front of me. Then I lowered my head and *rushed* at the mummy with all the speed I could muster.

I smashed the point of the pyramid into his back.

He groaned and spun around.

And I shoved the pyramid hard into his chest.

His arms flew up. His head tilted to one side. He staggered backward. His legs bumped against the side of the case—and he fell in.

I gripped the heavy pyramid in front of me. My whole body trembled. I watched the mummy fall into the case.

"*Cathy* . . . *Unnnnnh* . . . *Cathy* . . ."

Arragotus landed hard on his back. But it looked as if he was going to get up again.

I saw the writing on the side of the mummy's case. Shannon said she read it, and that's when the mummy came to life. The same thing that happened with Slappy last night. I had a hunch. It was worth a shot. I shouted the words out loud.

The mummy uttered a groan. Then I watched his body flatten against the stone bottom. He didn't move. The words had put him back to sleep.

I let the heavy model pyramid fall to the floor.

"Wow. Cathy, are you okay?" Shannon rushed forward and wrapped me in a hug.

"I . . . I think so," I stammered. I couldn't stop my legs from trembling, my heart from pounding.

"That was *awesome*," Logan said. He shook his head. "I can't believe you defeated an ancient mummy!"

"I can't believe it either," I said, still struggling to catch my breath.

I turned and saw Dad come walking over to us. He was still rubbing the back of his head. But his eyes looked clear and normal again.

"I . . . I think I was knocked out," he said, his voice hoarse. "I'm so sorry I couldn't help you."

"Are you okay?" Shannon asked him.

He nodded. "Yeah. I think so." He turned and gazed into the mummy case. "But what are we going to do about this guy?"

Arragotus lay still. He looked dead, as he had looked for thousands of years.

"This is impossible. But it really happened," Dad continued to stare at the mummy, stunned. "It's the same thing that happened with the dummy last night!"

"We told you, but you didn't believe us!" Logan said.

"We have to cancel the overnight," Dad said sadly. "We can't take the chance someone might get hurt."

"But, Dad—" Shannon started.

"This is a very angry mummy," Dad said. He gazed into the case. "No wonder those people were so willing to get rid of him." He rubbed his head. "If Arragotus wakes up again, he's too dangerous. It's just too big a risk."

I could see how disappointed Dad was. We all were. But I knew he was right.

"We have to tell everyone in your class," Dad said. "Right away." He turned from the mummy case and started out of the room. "They are coming on a bus together. I'll call the driver. Or maybe your teacher. Everyone has to be stopped before they come here. We—"

We all gasped as a loud buzzer rang out.

The doorbell at the front of the museum.

I heard footsteps. Voices out in the hall. Laughter.

I turned and gazed down the hall.

"Now what, Dad? They're already here!"

18

Shouts and laughs rang off the high walls as my class poured into the museum. Mrs. Uris, my teacher, was herding everyone through the hall.

Dad came up behind me and placed a hand on my shoulder. "I don't know what to do," he said. "Should I just tell everyone to turn around and go home?"

I glanced back into the mummy room. Arragotus was out cold. Dead again. He hadn't moved.

"Everyone will be so upset if we cancel," I said. "And we'll be careful. *No way* we'll read those words."

"We'd better move the boys' cots out of the mummy room," Dad said. "Why risk one of them reading the words on the mummy case?"

"If the mummy comes back to life, I'll tickle him to death!" Shannon exclaimed. She laughed and started to tickle me under the chin.

I knew she was just trying to look brave. But I didn't want to be tickled at just that moment.

I jerked around and pushed her hand away. "Stop it, Shannon. And don't tickle any of my friends. No one likes it."

She made a phony pouty face. "You're mean."

I hurried to greet my friends. Most of them had been to my dad's museum before. Most of them shared my attitude that it was kind of baby-ish and not too scary. But they didn't come for the scares. They came to party all night.

"What's that weird smell?" my friend Scott asked, sniffing the air. "Smells like an old closet."

I realized he was smelling the ancient odor left by the mummy. A chill rolled down my back. I glanced to the mummy room. Nothing moving there.

I knew I'd be tense about the mummy all night.

"There's a lot of old stuff here that, well, smells old," I told Scott.

He grinned at me. "Does your dad still have that three-legged dinosaur skeleton?"

I nodded. "Three legs are better than none."

"Is he going to try to scare us tonight?" Scott asked.

"You know my dad," I replied.

Scott snickered. "Hope I don't scream like a baby."

We both laughed. But my laugh was fake. I was thinking about Arragotus. *If he comes to life again, we'll all be screaming.*

It didn't take long to get everyone settled. Then we gathered beneath the wide stairs in the front hall. "Sit down, everyone. Get comfortable," Dad said. "I want you all to have a scary good time at my Haunted Horror Museum."

"Oooh, scary," someone murmured. "I'm shaking."

Some kids laughed.

Dad ignored them. "I'm going to start out by telling you a true story."

"Can we see the new mummy?" Ashli Munroe shouted. A few kids murmured their agreement.

"Later," Dad said. "I want to tell you a story first."

Dad planned to start in the mummy room. But I guess he had changed his mind. Was he stalling? Waiting to see if Arragotus would come walking down the hall?

"How old is the dinosaur skeleton?" LeBron Harkness called out. "Is it as old as Mrs. Uris?"

That made everyone laugh. Mrs. Uris sat in a chair against the back wall. She jumped to her feet and shook a fist at LeBron. "I'm only thirty-six. Does that make me a dinosaur?" She has a good sense of humor. That's why we liked to tease her.

"The dinosaur is older than Mrs. Uris," Dad said. "It's at least seventy million years old. And do you know where it was found?"

"In Scott's backyard?" someone shouted.

Scott's backyard is famous because it's like a

junkyard, cluttered with all kinds of old car parts and metal scraps and rusted engines and stuff.

"Actually, it was found in a field in Montana," Dad said. "Did you know there were dinosaurs in Montana?"

"So can we see the mummy?" Ashli repeated.

Dad grinned at her. "The mummy is taking his dinner break."

He settled back against the wall of the stairway and began to tell his story. "A lot of people ask me why I call this place the Haunted Horror Museum," he said. "Is it really haunted? The answer is yes."

A few kids snickered. Shannon, who sat beside Dad, rolled her eyes. I glanced down the hall toward the mummy room. Nothing going on down there.

"Maybe you can tell this museum was originally an old mansion," Dad continued. "It has thirty-five rooms, three floors, and was actually built in the early 1800s."

"Older than me!" Mrs. Uris chimed in, and we laughed again.

"The mansion was built by a very wealthy family whose last name was Tyler. The Tyler family had seven children," Dad continued. "So all the rooms were filled, with bedrooms for the parents and the children, and there were even a few guest rooms for the family's relatives to stay in."

Dad took a pause. A hush had fallen over the

front hall as we all became interested in his story.

I was surprised I'd never heard it before. Was it true? Was he making it up as he went along? I knew he wanted to keep us all away from the mummy room until he could be sure the mummy was really dead again.

"Tyler fell into trouble," Dad continued. "His business went bankrupt. He owed the bank thousands of dollars. Sadly, he realized he could not keep his house. It was only days until the bank would take it from him."

Dad paused. No one moved or spoke.

"He was desperate," Dad said. "He hired a wagon to carry him and his family out of town. His plan was to travel to his mother's house in Ohio. The wagon arrived in the middle of the night. Tyler was frantic to get away before the bankers could have him arrested. The family hurried into the wagon, taking few of their possessions."

Dad paused again, then said, "And now I'm coming to the tragic part of the story."

"You mean they were caught? They didn't make it?" LeBron demanded.

"No, they made it out of town," Dad said. "The wagon carried them several miles ... The horse racing at top speed. But many miles later, they made a horrifying discovery. In their panic, they had left one of the kids behind. Five-year-old William."

A few kids gasped. Most everyone remained silent.

"William was left in this big mansion all alone," Dad said. "His room was right up these stairs." Dad pointed. "Can you imagine being abandoned by your parents in the middle of the night and left all alone in this huge house?"

"Did his parents come back for him?" I asked.

Dad took a long moment to answer. "They did. They had the driver turn the wagon around and they came back. It was afternoon of the next day, and . . . they were heartbroken. They couldn't find William anywhere. There was no sign of him. No sign at all."

"You mean he just disappeared?" Shannon asked.

Dad nodded. "Vanished. Vanished forever. Until now."

"Until now?" Ashli said.

Dad nodded again. "I found him. I found William when I bought this house and turned it into a museum."

"Huh?"

"Excuse me?"

A few kids muttered their surprise.

"William must have died in the house," Dad explained. "And he stayed to haunt it. The boy haunts this museum. I have seen him. I have seen him clearly coming down these stairs from his room."

81

"He's a real ghost?" Shannon asked. "You've seen a real ghost? William's ghost?"

Dad nodded. Then he raised his eyes to the stairs. "Oh my goodness!" he exclaimed. "He must have heard me telling his story. There he is."

Some kids cried out. Some jumped to their feet, backing up in alarm.

I tried to focus, not believing my eyes. A boy . . . a boy dressed all in white . . . His face as white as his shirt . . . white as cake flour . . . A boy so pale and ghostly . . .

Holding on to the banister with a milk-white hand, he started from the top of the stairway, gazing straight ahead, and came floating down the stairs.

19

Kids screamed. I saw Mrs. Uris jump up from her chair, her eyes bulging. I held my breath, my heart pounding.

The ghostly boy was halfway down the wide staircase when I caught the smile on Dad's face. And I recognized Logan.

Logan dressed in white. Logan's face behind a layer of thick white makeup.

A few seconds later, other kids recognized him, too. And the screams turned to laughter.

Dad's grin grew wider. "Some of you don't think this museum is scary," he said. "I thought maybe Logan and I could change your mind."

Kids began to settle back on the floor. "Logan, you need to get out in the sun more!" Candy Morales called out.

"How do I get this stuff off my face?" Logan asked my dad. "It's like an inch thick and it itches."

"Use a shovel!" someone shouted.

"I feel like a mummy," Logan complained.

That made me glance down the hall. Nothing going on. Arragotus was enjoying being dead again, thank goodness.

Dad pointed back up the stairs. "Use the restroom up there, Logan. It will come right off with water and paper towels."

Logan turned and went back up the stairs, two at a time. It took a while to get everyone quiet again.

Aaron Riggles raised his hand. Aaron is a great guy. I love his red hair and freckles. He's totally cute.

He hangs out with Logan a lot, and he lives a few blocks down the street from me. "Mr. O'Connor," he said, "is that story true at all? Did his family really leave him all alone in this house?"

Dad shook his head. "No. Sorry, Aaron. I made up the story. Actually, the town barber lived here for many years."

Aaron frowned. I could see he was disappointed by Dad's answer. He wanted the William story to be true.

"Actually, the barber story is pretty interesting," Dad said. "He also had to leave town very quickly. He was giving the mayor a shave, and he accidentally cut off the man's ear."

Dad reached into his shirt pocket. He pulled out a human ear and held it up so everyone could see it. "Here it is," he said.

A few kids gasped. Some others laughed.

"You can't fool us again," Aaron said, shaking his head.

Dad sighed. "Oh well. I thought it was worth a try." He tucked the ear back into his pocket.

He climbed to his feet. "I guess it's time," he said. "I know you are all waiting to see the museum's new mummy."

He turned to Shannon and me when he said that. I could see he was still worried about bringing everyone into the mummy room.

"The mummy, Arragotus, was about to become an Egyptian prince," Dad explained. "But he died on the morning he was to be crowned. The legend goes that his anger at being cheated lived on inside him—even after he was mummified."

Dad motioned for everyone to follow him. Shannon and I exchanged glances as we started down the long hall.

"He is a very angry mummy," Dad said as he walked. "So do not touch him or make him angrier in any way. Do not lean over the side. Whatever you do, do *not* touch the sleeping prince."

I stepped up beside Aaron and Ashli. "This is cool," Aaron said. "Your dad is funny."

"He sure likes scaring people," Ashli said.

I felt a chill at the back of my neck. *You don't know how scary it can get around here*, I thought.

"I think mummies are sick," Ashli said. "I

mean, every time I see a mummy, I just think, 'There's a dead person inside there.' Yuck."

We were nearly to the mummy room. I could feel my muscles tighten in dread. I crossed my fingers. *Please—stay dead, Arragotus.*

Candy Morales and a few other kids were walking ahead of everyone. I watched them step into the mummy room.

And then I froze as I heard Candy scream: "It's ALIVE! I don't believe it. It's ALIVE!"

20

I took off running. I pushed a few kids aside and got to the door at the same time as Dad.

I stopped, my heart thudding, and saw Candy and her friends laughing.

No sign that the mummy had moved from his resting place.

Candy grinned at my dad. "You're not the only scary person here!" she exclaimed. She and her friends laughed some more.

Candy squinted at Dad and me. "I think you actually believed me."

"No way," I lied. "But you're a good actress, Candy."

Dad was still catching his breath. Kids jammed into the room. The blue lights cast a dim glow. The walls were dark wood. It was supposed to be a creepy place, but tonight it was way too creepy for me.

A hush fell over the room. Kids stepped up to the case one by one to study the ancient prince.

A lot of crazy movies have been made about mummies coming to life and terrorizing people. So to a lot of kids, mummies are kind of a joke.

But when you stand beside a real mummy, and you see that it's a real person who once walked around, all wrapped up in ancient cloth and stuck inside ancient tar . . . When you see a real mummy close-up, it gives you the creeps.

My arms were still sore from lifting that heavy model pyramid. And the pictures of the groaning, grunting, staggering mummy played over and over again in my mind.

I had my arms crossed tightly in front of me. This was supposed to be a party, but I wished it would just end.

Did I really fight a living mummy?

And was it less than an hour ago?

I saw Shannon gazing at the shield against the wall. I knew she was having thoughts like mine.

I walked back out into the hall. I waited for everyone to have their turn with the mummy. When I felt a hand on my shoulder, I nearly jumped up to the ceiling.

I spun around and saw Logan.

"Sorry," he said. "I called to you, but you didn't hear me." He still had a few spots of white makeup behind his ears.

"You gave everyone a good scare back there," I said, pointing to the staircase.

"I saw that dummy upstairs," Logan said. "He's

in a glass case. And there was a big lock on the case, so it should be safe."

"Good," I said. "We don't need anything else coming to life tonight."

"The dummy is creepy enough when he *isn't* alive," Logan said. "The big grin on his face is seriously sick."

"The only good thing is," I said, "there's *no way* the dummy will come to life. That's one thing we don't have to worry about."

21

Everyone was hungry, so we took a break from the scares and made our way to the basement café and ate tons of pizza. Dad had set up a soft-serve ice-cream machine, and everyone liked making their own cones.

I sat at a table across from Ashli and Candy, and they kept telling me what an awesome party it was and how cool it was to stay up all night. They laughed about how serious Dad was and how hard he tried to scare everyone.

It was difficult to concentrate on what they were saying. Their voices kept fading away. I was thinking about the mummy, watching the stairway. Thinking the mummy would come roaring down to attack everyone at any minute.

Talk about tense.

After the food, we teamed up for the scavenger hunt. Shannon announced there were at least a hundred insects in amber hidden around the museum. The team that collected the most would win a prize.

"We did this at my fifth birthday party!" LeBron complained.

"Well, you're doing it again," Shannon told him. "Only this time it's harder because I hid the amber stones." She passed out little bags to put the stones in.

Logan asked if I wanted to be his partner, and I said yes. I took a bag from Shannon and turned to go upstairs to start the hunt. But she chased after Logan and me and stopped us in the hall.

"Can I be on your team?" she asked.

"Of course not," I said.

She made her pouty face. "Why not?"

Logan answered for me. "Because you hid the stones, Shannon. You already know where they are. It would be cheating."

Her pout changed to a sly smile. "But I could help you win," she said in a whisper.

"No way," I said. "You're supposed to be working, remember? Helping out?"

Shannon wiggled her fingers in front of my face. "If you don't let me come with you, I'll tickle you to death." She reached up and started tickling my neck.

I pushed her away. "Go tickle the mummy," I snapped.

I realized at once it was a bad joke.

Shannon's smile faded. Her chin quivered. "Can I tell you a secret?" she said in a whisper. "I'm kind of scared. Because of the mummy. I don't really want to be by myself."

I hesitated. "Well—"

Dad's shout interrupted. "Hey, Shannon. Come help me. We have to clean up the food tables."

"You'll be safe with Dad," I said. "And then you can hang out with me later."

Her chin was still quivering. "Tonight was supposed to be fun, you know? Not scary like this."

"The mummy is dead," Logan told her. "He won't come to life again."

Did he really believe that? Or was he just trying to make my sister feel better?

Logan and I started to climb the stairs to the first floor. "Your sister looks really terrified," he said.

"Aren't *you*?" I replied with a shudder.

Kids were splitting up, heading in different directions. Voices echoed off the high walls.

"Found one!" a girl shouted from the werewolf room.

That room is across the hall from the mummy room. Dad has a frightening stuffed wolf in there, standing on two legs on a tall pedestal with its teeth bared. I know a little secret about the wolf. It isn't real. The fur is actually made from a shag rug we had in the basement.

"Are there any stones in the mummy room?"

someone shouted to Shannon. "Did you hide any in the mummy case?"

"No. No way," I heard Shannon reply. "None in the mummy room. Stay out of there!"

"There's one under that stuffed snake," I heard a girl call out from around the corner.

"I saw it first," another girl said.

"But I *grabbed* it first."

Logan pointed to the stairway. "Too crowded down here. Let's go to the second floor. I know Shannon hid some up there."

I agreed. I led the way upstairs. The air was warmer up here and kind of steamy. We walked past the Garden of Venus Flytraps. Behind that, bats fluttered in their dark-windowed sanctuary.

The bats are the only living creatures in Dad's museum. He spends a lot of time taking care of them. They definitely are my favorite thing in the horror museum.

I've done a bunch of studies about bats for school. One out of every five mammals on earth is a bat. I think that's pretty cool.

"I don't see any amber stones," Logan said. "Maybe I'm wrong. Maybe your sister didn't put any up here."

"Yes, she did," I said. "Keep looking."

We walked by the Frankenstein's Monster display. Dad has posters from the original *Frankenstein* movie and a mask of the monster that's seriously terrifying.

"Hey—" I spotted something glowing near the mask. An amber stone. I picked it up from the floor and gazed at the tiny black insect inside. "Got you, little bug," I said.

I handed it to Logan and he tucked it into our bag.

Against the back wall, Slappy the dummy grinned at us from inside his glass display case. Logan shook his head. "I can't believe someone just dumped that thing in back of the museum."

"Dad has a pretty big lock on that case," I said. "Slappy won't be getting out to terrorize everyone."

Logan sighed. "If only there was a lock on the mummy room . . ."

I stopped when I heard a loud *thud*. From downstairs. The sound was followed by a startled cry.

I knew instantly what it was.

The mummy was out. The mummy was on the loose.

SLAPPY HERE, EVERYONE.

Hey, I love the Haunted Horror Museum. My favorite thing? The whale eyeball.

Too bad it isn't there anymore. I had it for breakfast.

It was a little dry. I probably should have cooked it first!

Why was I locked up in a glass case? I know people like to admire me. But I don't think I should be locked up.

After all, I'm not a scary guy. I don't know where people got that mistaken idea. I'm a *simple* guy. I just want one thing.

I want everyone I meet to follow every order I give!

What's scary about that?!

Hahahaha.

22

I raced down the stairs, taking them two at a time. I saw a crowd of kids gathered at the end of the hall.

No sign of the mummy. Where was he?

Shannon saw me and came running down the hall. "It's okay," she said. She must have seen the horrified look on my face.

"Wh-what happened?" I stammered.

"The Stephen King statue," she said, pointing. "Scott accidentally knocked it over."

I let out a long whoosh of air. My heart was pounding. "The statue?"

Shannon nodded. "I hid one of the amber stones between Stephen King's legs. Scott grabbed for it and—"

I saw Dad tilting the statue back onto its feet. "Nothing broken!" he shouted. "All okay. It's cast iron!"

He turned to Scott. "It's a good thing you didn't

knock over Edgar Allan Poe. That statue is made of porcelain. Poor Edgar would be in pieces."

A few minutes later, we gathered in the main hall. Dad disappeared up the front staircase while Shannon counted the amber stones.

Scott and Aaron were the winning team, with six stones. Their prize was two white plastic skulls filled with jellybeans.

Shannon piled the stones on a shelf on the back wall.

"Now Shannon and I are going to show you the newest attraction at the Haunted Horror Museum." Dad walked into the room with the dummy. I gasped as he sat down and placed him on his lap.

"Dad! Wait a minute!" I cried. I ran up to him. "You locked the dummy away, remember?" I said, whispering so the others couldn't hear. "He's dangerous. Dad, we warned you last night. Why did you bring him down here?"

"I had to," Dad whispered back. "The party is getting dull. That scavenger hunt was too baby-ish. I can see that your friends are bored."

"But, Dad—!" I cried.

"I'll be careful," Dad said. "Really. I'll be careful with him, Cathy. Go sit down. I promise it'll be okay."

I stood staring at him with my mouth hanging open. I couldn't believe he'd take such a big risk just to make sure kids were entertained.

But . . . that's my dad.

I had no choice. I turned and sat down in the back row of kids.

Dad held the dummy up so everyone could see it. "I want you to meet my new friend," he said.

I heard a loud gasp. Aaron leaped to his feet. He pointed at the dummy with a trembling finger. "That dummy—" he started. "Where did you get him?"

Dad squinted at Aaron. "Is there a problem?"

Aaron's eyes were wide with surprise. "Is that dummy's name Slappy?" he demanded.

"Why, yes," Dad said. "Yes, it is. How do you know that, Aaron?"

"P-put him away!" Aaron stammered. He kept pointing at it, as if accusing it. "I'm serious, Mr. O'Connor. Get rid of him."

Dad had been sitting on a folding chair with Slappy on his lap. Now he climbed to his feet and held the dummy in front of him. "Calm down, Aaron. He's just a puppet."

Kids buzzed and murmured. Everyone looked very confused. Mrs. Uris had her hands pressed to the sides of her face.

"I had that dummy in my house," Aaron said. "He was given to me. A puppeteer gave him to me. He . . . he's dangerous, Mr. O'Connor. He's . . . evil."

Dad squinted at Aaron. "You had Slappy at your house? Are you serious?"

"My dad got rid of him," Aaron said. "He was evil, and my dad put him in the car. He never told us what he did with him. But—"

"You mean your dad was the one who dropped him at our back door?" Dad asked. "He dropped him here and then sped away."

"Probably," Aaron said. "I don't know. I just know he had to get him out of our house."

Dad held Slappy out at arm's length and studied him. "You really get around, Slappy," he said.

"Please, Mr. O'Connor—" Aaron's voice cracked.

Dad motioned for Aaron to sit down. "Relax," Dad said. "Take a seat. Let's give this dummy a test run. Let's see if you're right, Aaron. I promise I'll be careful."

I felt the muscles tighten at the back of my neck. I knew Aaron was right. Why didn't Dad listen to him and just put the dummy away?

He had a small stack of papers at his feet. He reached down and fumbled through them. "Slappy comes with a story," Dad told everyone. "He was made by an evil wizard out of coffin wood. That's what it says on one of these sheets. If I can just find the right one . . ."

He shuffled through the papers again.

I could feel myself growing more tense by the second.

A hush had fallen over the room. No one moved. Everyone was watching Dad in silence. Only Aaron kept shaking his head, muttering to himself.

"Here," Dad said, pulling up a sheet of paper. He settled back down with Slappy on his lap. "According to the legend, if someone shouts these words out loud, Slappy will come to life."

Dad leaned forward. "Should we do it? You tell me. Should we do it?"

Aaron was the first to answer. "No! Don't! Please—don't!"

A few kids shouted yes. Most didn't answer. Mrs. Uris still had her hands pressed to her face.

I ran up to Dad. "What are you *doing*?"

"Cathy, I'm not going to read the words," Dad whispered. "I'm just playing here. You know. Trying to make things scary. Don't worry."

"You're sure?" I demanded.

Dad nodded.

I started to back away—and I accidentally brushed the paper in his hand. He made a grab for it, but it floated out over the kids.

I saw Ashli grab it. And before I could warn her ... before I could scream at her to stop ... *she held the paper up and read the words!*

"ABASEEGO MODARO LAMADOROS CREBEN!"

The words rang in my ears. My mind started to spin.

Were those the right words?

23

The dummy didn't open his eyes. He didn't move.

Everyone watched in silence.

Dad turned to Ashli. "Hand me that paper. You shouldn't have read those words out loud."

A few kids laughed.

"It's just a dummy," LeBron called out. "Did you really think it would jump up and start to dance?"

More kids laughed. Ari Moone and David Palmer jumped up and started to dance, stiff-legged like dummies.

Dad leaned over to take the paper from Ashli—and dropped the dummy on its head. The wooden head made a loud *clonk* as it hit the stone floor.

That got kids laughing and hooting. But Aaron jumped to his feet, his expression serious and frightened. "Don't make Slappy mad!" he cried. "I'm serious. Don't make him mad!"

Kids laughed.

"Aaron, we already know you're a weirdo freak!" a boy yelled. "Why do you want to prove it again?"

More laughter.

Dad lifted the dummy off the floor and dusted off the top of his head with the palm of his hand. "He doesn't look too mad," Dad said. "He doesn't look alive at all."

"Dad, those might be the wrong words," I said.

Dad shuffled through the stack of papers on his lap. "All of this is a mess. There are papers from my desk mixed in here."

"How about *these* words?" Ari shouted. "Yabba dabba doo!"

That got a big laugh.

"How about Scooby Dooby Doo?" someone shouted.

"Wacka wacka wacka!"

"Dumbledore! Dumbledore!"

The big front hall erupted in echoing voices as everyone shouted out their ideas for magic words. Kids laughed and jumped around and called out their funny words.

I watched Aaron. He was the only one in my class who wasn't enjoying the shouts and laughter. He had backed to the wall and was standing near Mrs. Uris, his eyes down.

Aaron was a great guy. Usually a lot of fun. I wondered what happened at his house. Slappy must have come to life. But what horrible thing did he do?

Dad stood up and swung the dummy over his shoulder. He waited for the shouts to die down. "I'm going upstairs to put Slappy back in his case," he announced. "Crank up the music. Everyone have fun."

I watched him start to climb the staircase. The dummy bobbed on his shoulder. Its head kept bumping Dad's back as he climbed.

I had my eye on Aaron. I turned and made my way through the crowd toward him. But a hand on my shoulder stopped me.

It was Shannon. "I'm glad that dummy didn't come to life. He's evil—and Dad knows it. Why did he bring it down and tease everyone with it?"

"Sometimes Dad goes overboard when he has an audience at the museum," I said.

Shannon nodded. "I'm going downstairs. I'm getting more ice cream," she said. She hurried away.

Kids were talking and laughing. Ari and David were doing their dummy dance again.

I stepped up beside Aaron. He still stood against the wall, his eyes lowered to the floor. His red hair fell over his forehead. His hands were shoved into his jeans pockets.

"What's up with you?" I asked.

He jumped. He hadn't seen me step up to him.

"Your dad should listen to me," Aaron said. "I wasn't making a joke."

"You had the dummy at your house?"

He nodded. "You remember. That puppeteer who came to school last week. Mandrake the Great."

"Yes, I remember," I said. "His puppets were pretty funny."

"Well, he gave me Slappy," Aaron said. "I saw him leaving after school, and I went over to him. You know. To tell him I liked his show. And he gave me the dummy."

I squinted at Aaron. "He gave it to you? For free? Just like that?"

"Yeah. I didn't realize he wanted to get rid of it. I mean, he was *desperate* to get rid of it."

"Because?"

"Because Slappy is evil, Cathy. He ruined my house. He threw up this horrible green puke. It just poured and poured from his mouth. Like a volcano. He covered our house in sickening green puke."

My mouth dropped open. "Yuck," I murmured. "How awful."

"The dummy has powers," Aaron continued in a voice just above a whisper. "He has evil powers, Cathy. And he's totally sick. If he gets angry . . ." His voice trailed off.

"But he's asleep," I said. "Dad is putting him back in his case."

"What if he wakes up?" Aaron demanded, his eyes widening in fright. "What if Slappy comes to life, Cathy? He could hurt people. He could destroy this museum."

"Well, Dad is going to lock him back up," I said. "The dummy won't be able to get out of his display case."

"That's not enough," Aaron replied. "You should find the right sheet of paper with the right words on it. The words to bring Slappy to life. And you should rip the paper into a thousand pieces."

I stared hard at him. I didn't know what to say. "Let me think about it," I said finally. I squeezed his shoulder. "Try to relax, Aaron. Try to have a good time. I think we'll all be okay."

He lowered his eyes to the floor again and didn't reply.

I turned away and started back to the other kids. But something down the hall caught my eye.

Something moved at the far end of the long hall. I squinted hard, waiting for my eyes to focus.

And then I let out a cry when I saw the mummy.

Arragotus poked his head out of the room, then staggered stiff-legged into the hall.

24

My breath caught in my throat. The voices of my friends faded from my ears, and I was suddenly surrounded by an eerie silence.

I knew instantly what had happened. I suddenly realized what the words Ashli had shouted were. Those words ... *They were the words to bring the mummy to life.*

The papers from Dad's desk ... They got mixed up with the dummy's papers.

And now here was the mummy, his thick wrapped feet sliding and scraping on the stone floor as he began to stagger down the long hallway.

I spun around. Did anyone else see him?

Not yet.

Some kids had discovered the mask collection. They had pulled them out of their display case and were trying them on. And taking selfies in them.

I fought back my fear. I tried to think clearly. *What can I do? How can I stop him?*

The mummy moved slowly toward us. His arms hung by his sides. His head was lowered and it was aimed directly ahead.

I glanced back to the stairway. No sign of Dad. He was still upstairs.

Where was Shannon? I remembered she had gone to the basement to help herself to ice cream.

My mind was zigzagging all over the place. I was quickly learning how total panic keeps you from thinking straight.

As the mummy came closer, he raised one arm in the air. Another cry escaped my lips as I realized what he was doing. He was pointing at me!

"*Cathy . . . Cathy . . . Cathy . . .*"

Noooo. Oh no. Hearing my name again from deep in that ancient creature made me freeze in horror.

He remembered me.

He remembered how I had bashed him with that armored shield. How I had knocked him back into his case with the model pyramid. He remembered I was the one who put him back to sleep.

If only I could get that big armored shield now, maybe I could protect my friends and drive the mummy back. But the shield was in the mummy room. I'd have to run past him to get there.

And I knew he would stop me.

I glanced around frantically, looking for another weapon. Nothing in sight. Nothing I could use.

"*Cathy* . . ."

The mummy kept his arm raised in front of him, his hand trained on me as he lurched forward. He was coming for me. Coming for revenge.

I had to act. I had to do *something*.

A scream shook me from my frozen panic. It was Ashli. She saw the mummy. She was the first to see him moving steadily down the hall toward us.

Other kids followed her gaze. Kids ripped off their masks and turned to stare at the approaching figure.

I heard gasps and murmurs. Another scream. Mrs. Uris jumped to her feet, eyes wide with alarm.

Everyone saw him now. Everyone froze and gaped as the mummy drew near.

And then I heard someone laugh. I turned and saw LeBron pointing and laughing. More kids broke into loud laughter.

And then to my shock, they *began running toward the mummy*!

Laughing, shaking their heads, they stampeded past me, heading to the approaching mummy.

"Wait! Stop!" I screamed.

But my voice was drowned out by the thunder of footsteps and cries of laughter.

"Stop!" I shrieked. What were they DOING?

Scott must have heard me. He turned back to me. "Come on, Cathy," he shouted. "We all know it's your DAD!"

25

I screamed some more, but no one paid attention. My friends swarmed around the mummy, admiring it.

"Awesome costume," someone said.

"Ewwww. Mr. O'Connor, you even *smell* ancient!"

The mummy stopped for a long moment. He turned his head from side to side, as if confused by the warm greeting.

A low grunt came from deep inside his chest. He lurched forward and grabbed Candy.

"Hey—!" she cried out in surprise. "Let go. You're hurting me, Mr. O'Connor."

The mummy whipped his arm around and spun Candy into the wall. She uttered another surprised cry. "That isn't funny—"

And then I heard a familiar voice call from the stairway. "What's up? What's going on?"

My dad appeared halfway down the stairs.

"*Rrrowwwrrr.*" The mummy uttered a nasty growl.

Kids screamed. Stumbling, bumping into each other, eyes wide with horror, they realized they'd made a big mistake. And now they all struggled to back away from the terrifying figure.

With another growl, the mummy lowered his shoulder into a glass display case filled with paperback horror books. The glass shattered and the books went flying.

More screams.

"Arragotus—stop!" Dad shouted. He hurtled down the stairs and ran toward everyone, waving both hands. "Back away, everyone! This is real. It isn't a joke!"

Now the stampede moved in the other direction. Everyone scrambled to get away from the raging mummy.

"Rrraaaarrrgh!"

With a roar from deep in his chest, Arragotus smashed another display case. Glass flew across the hall. Kids howled in panic. "Is this really happening?" someone cried.

"Is this another joke to scare us?"

"Oooh. It smells so awful! It *reeks*!"

The mummy turned toward me. He stopped, as if remembering his mission.

"Unnnnh." An ugly grunt burst from his throat. And then my name, like another groan.

"*Cathy. Cathy.*" He moved toward me again, just a few feet away now, dragging one foot heavily on the floor, then the other.

"Dad! Do something!" I screamed. Again, I scanned the hall searching for a weapon.

Shannon appeared at the top of the steps to the basement. She had a chocolate ice-cream cone in her hand. I saw the look of confusion on her face. And then I saw her eyes go wide as she saw the mummy roaring down the hall.

The cone fell from her hand and made a loud *splat* on the floor. She came running toward me. "Cathy, he's . . . he's alive again! Oh no!"

The mummy had everyone pinned at the end of the hallway. No way to get around him. No chance of getting to the exit doors.

"Did anyone call 911?" Mrs. Uris shouted over their cries.

"We're trapped!"

"The mummy will get us all!"

"Somebody—help!"

Screams of panic rang out down the hall.

Dad stood frozen in panic for a long moment. I could see he was struggling to think clearly.

"Wait! I know what to do!" Dad yelled. "I can stop him. I know what to do!"

26

Another crash of shattering glass. The mummy knocked over another display case. He ripped a large painting of Dracula off the wall and shoved a hard fist through it.

Dad turned to Mrs. Uris. "Take as many of the children upstairs as you can and hide," he said. "There are lots of rooms. Spread out."

She nodded and a group of students hurried after her.

"We're not going, Dad," I said. "We have to save you!"

Dad turned to Shannon and me. "Okay. I'm thinking about the words that brought the mummy to life..." he said breathlessly. "I think...maybe...if we read them again, they will put him back to sleep."

"That's right!" I cried. How could I have forgotten? "Dad—do it! We can't get past him to read them off the mummy case. But you have the paper."

He blinked. "Huh? No. I don't have it. I'm pretty sure . . ."

"Ashli had it," I said. "But she returned it to you, Dad. After she read the words. I saw her."

I glanced back. The mummy was close. I couldn't see his eyes because they were covered in gauze and tar. But I knew he was looking at me. Coming for me. Coming for his revenge.

He stretched his arms out, ready . . . ready to grab me.

"Where is the paper with the words?" Dad frantically searched his pants pockets. "Is it on my desk?" He didn't wait for an answer. He turned and took off, running toward his office.

A few moments later, Dad came running back. I didn't see a sheet of paper in his hand. His face was bright red. "Dad—" I started.

"I can't find it," he said. "It wasn't anywhere. I don't know—"

My scream cut off his words.

I let out a shrill scream of terror as I felt rough hands grab me from behind. Then a hard hand wrapped around my throat.

The mummy had me . . . had me . . . had me in his grip.

27

Choking me. The dry, hard fingers tightened around my throat. I struggled to breathe.

Kids shrieked in horror. Loud cries filled my ears over the roar of my pulsing blood.

Dad leaped at the mummy. He tackled him around the waist and tried to bring him down. But Arragotus stayed on his feet, and his hands didn't move from my neck.

Dad grappled with him. His hands wrapped around the mummy's waist.

"Rrrrrrrr." The mummy snarled as he fought Dad. I felt myself growing weak. I took in a gasping breath of air.

Dizzy. I was dizzy now. The room was spinning around me.

The tight fingers on my throat ... can't breathe ... fading ... I felt myself fading.

His hands were so strong. His head loomed over me. I could feel his stare through the thick web of cloth and tar. And the smell . . . the ancient odor . . . so sour . . . so sickening.

"No! I will not let you do this!" A sudden burst of anger shot through me. I raised both hands and grabbed the mummy's wrists. Then I shot my foot up in a ferocious kick.

I kicked the ancient creature hard in the belly. Raised my foot again and kicked him in the shin.

Arragotus groaned and slid back in surprise and pain. His hands lifted from my throat.

I sucked in a deep breath. Another. The air felt so cool. My heart pounded so hard I could hear it.

Dad still had the mummy around the waist. Now he swung his body into him—and they both toppled to the floor. My dad landed on top of Arragotus. He grabbed the mummy's arms and tried to pin him to the floor.

My neck throbbed. I could still feel the mummy fingers tightening around me.

As I watched in horror, struggling to catch my breath, I realized someone was tugging on my sleeve.

I turned.

Aaron?

"Cathy—here." He shoved the dummy into my hands.

I gasped. "Aaron—what are you thinking? You brought him downstairs? Why?"

"I saw him when I went upstairs to hide. The dummy has powers," Aaron said. "Let's bring him to life. He can control the mummy. I know it. Maybe Slappy can put the mummy back to sleep."

Dad wrestled on the floor with the mummy. I knew there wasn't much time.

My brain was spinning. My heart was still pounding. I could still feel the mummy's hard fingers around my throat. I could still feel his rage, his anger.

I grabbed the dummy around the waist and raised him in front of me. Slappy weighed more than I'd imagined. His head and hands were made of some kind of heavy wood.

I held him tightly. Something about his wide grin . . . *An evil grin,* I thought. It sent a shiver to the back of my neck.

"The words," Aaron said. "We need the words to bring him to life."

"I don't know where they are!" I cried.

Dad had Arragotus pinned to the floor. But I knew he couldn't keep him down much longer.

"There they are!" Aaron exclaimed. He pulled a folded-up paper from the dummy's suit jacket pocket. "This has to be them," he said. He unfolded the paper. "Yes! The words. We have the words, Cathy. This is going to work. I know it will!"

"Okay. Okay. Let's do it," I said.

Aaron raised the sheet of paper. And shouted the words.

"KARRU MARRI ODONNA LOMA MOLONU KARRANO."

I crossed my fingers and gritted my teeth. *Please work. Please work.*

28

I gasped as Slappy leaped out of my arms and landed on his feet beside me. Everyone screamed in shock.

Aaron uttered a startled cry. He grabbed my arm and stared down at Slappy.

Slappy blinked a few times, his glassy eyes gazed around the scene. His mouth clicked up and down as if he were testing it.

Then his grin appeared to grow wider. He tossed back his head and laughed, a long, shrill, ugly laugh that made everyone who hadn't gone upstairs go silent.

"Well, well," he rasped. *"The world just got brighter. Slappy is here!"*

A hard chill made my body shudder. My dizziness made the whole museum hall spin.

Dad and the mummy stopped their frantic wrestling. The mummy raised his head to watch Slappy.

"You'd all better wear sunglasses!" Slappy

declared. *"I'm so bright, your head might explode!"*

Shannon gasped and pressed herself against the back wall.

"Don't applaud. Just bow down to your master!" Slappy exclaimed. He raised both hands in the air, as if he was celebrating a triumph.

"I know you're glad to see me," Slappy shouted. *"I heard your screams. But try to control your overwhelming love for me! Hahahaha!"*

"Hey, Aaron," Dad called out, entangled with the mummy. "Are you working that dummy? How are you doing that?"

"Who's working your *mouth?"* Slappy shouted back. *"And don't call me dummy, Dummy!"*

A hush fell over the long hall.

Dad rolled off the mummy. He climbed to his feet. He was drenched in sweat, his face bright red.

The mummy didn't move from the floor.

"I'm not working the dummy," Aaron told Dad. "We brought him alive. Slappy is alive now. He's real, everyone."

"It's going to be an educational night!" Slappy cried. *"You're all going to learn how to obey me! Hahahaha!"*

The mummy uttered a loud grunt. I sucked in my breath as he finally began to move. With great effort, he pushed himself to his feet.

I spun the dummy around. "Slappy, you have to help us," I said, my voice cracking. "That mummy—he's angry and out of control. We are all in danger. Can you help us? Please, Slappy. Do something. Help us."

The dummy's eyes locked on mine. He didn't reply for a moment. And then he screamed: "*Are you* kidding *me? Me help* you?"

"Please, Slappy—" I lost it. I grabbed him by the shoulders of his suit jacket and began to shake him. "Please help us!"

"*I* help *myself to whatever I want,*" he replied. "*That's the only kind of* helping *I ever do! Hahaha.*"

"Listen. I'm begging you—" I said.

I held on to his shoulders. I pleaded with him with my eyes.

I should have been watching the mummy. I didn't realize Arragotus had moved toward me.

Shannon started yelling. I turned to see why. Not in time. The mummy reached for me.

I opened my mouth to shout, but no sound came out.

With a growl, the mummy grabbed me again. Grabbed me around the waist with his two steel-hard hands . . . grabbed me and lifted me off the floor.

A sigh escaped my throat. I knew I was too weary. I didn't have the strength to fight him anymore.

What did he plan to do?

29

To my shock, the mummy opened his hands and let me drop back to the floor. He lurched past me and moved toward Slappy.

He wants the dummy—not me!

With a loud groan, Arragotus swung his right fist hard and fast at Slappy's head.

The dummy's legs folded like an accordion. Slappy ducked, and the mummy's punch missed him by inches.

Slappy turned to us. *"Hey,"* he shouted, *"who brought this toilet paper roll to life?"*

Snarling, the mummy dove forward. He shoved his head into the dummy's belly, knocking him down. Then Arragotus lifted Slappy high—and heaved him across the hall.

Slappy fell between Logan and me. We both reached down to help him to his feet.

Slappy ignored us and raised his eyes to the mummy. *"I get it!"* he shouted. *"You don't play well with others!"*

Moving with surprising speed, the mummy leaped at Slappy and grabbed him with one hand. Arragotus wrapped his hands around the dummy's ankles. Holding Slappy by the feet, he lifted him high.

"Careful of the shoes!" Slappy cried. *"It's hard to find an adult size two!"*

A roar burst from deep inside the ancient mummy. Arragotus held Slappy upside down and batted his head with a big fist. The mummy used Slappy as a punching bag, batting him again and again.

"Sorry, pal!" Slappy cried. *"I'm not into contact sports!"*

Arragotus slammed his fist hard into Slappy's wooden head. The punch made a *clonnnnnk* sound, and Slappy went flying.

Kids screamed and ducked out of the way. Slappy hit the far wall and collapsed to the floor. He didn't move for a long moment.

I turned to Logan. "Did the mummy *kill* him?"

Logan squinted at me. "Can you kill a dummy?"

Slappy finally climbed to his feet. His eyes locked on the mummy. *"Am I getting the feeling you don't want to be friends?"* he rasped.

Arragotus groaned and came staggering after Slappy. The mummy raised his fists, preparing to batter Slappy again.

But the dummy stood stiffly and narrowed his eyes at the attacking mummy. *"Say nighty-night* to everyone, *Band-Aid Butt!*" Slappy shouted. "*Trust me. You need your beauty rest. I'm putting you back to sleep!*"

The mummy took one more step, swinging his fists in front of him.

Slappy opened his eyes wide—and a red ray of light came shooting out of them. A powerful light beam that made the whole hallway glow with a pulsing red as if on fire.

Eyes wide, Slappy aimed the ray at the mummy's head.

Arragotus froze. His arms fell to his sides.

The ray flamed from Slappy's eyes. Brighter . . . brighter . . . casting the mummy in a blinding circle of light.

"*Nighty-night!*" Slappy shrieked. "*Unpleasant dreams!*"

30

I had to look away. The red ray was hurting my eyes. Beside me, Logan covered his face with his hands. Even with my eyes shut, I could still see the red glow pulsing on my eyelids.

When the glow faded, I opened my eyes.

Slappy stood in place, shaking his head, blinking his eyes.

The mummy didn't move. He stood frozen in place. Frozen by Slappy's powerful ray.

"Yes!" I cried. I pumped my fist above my head. "You did it! Slappy—you did it!"

We started to cheer.

But then the mummy rolled his head on his shoulders. He raised his arms over his head, stretching. And then with a roaring groan, Arragotus lurched toward Slappy as if nothing had happened.

"*I guess my ray didn't work on you,*" Slappy said calmly. "*I did give you a nice tan! Hahahaha!*"

"It's not funny," I murmured to Logan. "Slappy failed. Why is he making jokes?"

"M-maybe he has another plan," Logan stammered.

I screamed as the mummy swooped down and wrapped his hands around Slappy's legs again. He lifted the dummy off the floor, holding him upside down.

Arragotus raised him high, then brought the dummy down hard, smacking Slappy's head on the floor. He lifted him, then banged the head onto the floor. Again. Again.

Dad came running up behind me. "The dummy isn't going to be able to help," he said. "We have to get everyone out of here."

Slam slam slam.

The helpless dummy's arms hung limply down as the mummy continued to hold Slappy upside down and bang his head on the stone floor.

Slam.

"Is this what they mean by a slam dunk?" Slappy shouted.

Slam.

"This is getting boring!" the dummy cried. *"You've got to lighten up, Old Kleenex Face!"*

Slam.

"Maybe my prehistoric friend will teach you a lesson!" Slappy shouted.

He raised a hand and motioned to the end of the hall. Then he cried out some strange words I couldn't understand.

I heard a crash. A loud *thud.*

I turned in time to see a skull appear from the room at the end. The head of the dinosaur.

Bobbing on its three legs, the dinosaur skeleton came clattering down the hall. It tossed its giant head back. Its jaw moved up and down, stretching.

Shannon and Logan screamed. No one knew where to hide. We tried to crouch behind a display case. Aaron hid behind a statue. But no place was safe.

The mummy dropped Slappy to the floor and turned to see what the commotion was.

"My dinosaur friend is very hungry!" Slappy cried. *"You'll make a nice meal for him, Mummy Dearest. We've got to put some meat on his bones! Hahahaha."*

The foot bones hit the floor hard. The dinosaur head bounced. The jaws snapped. The enormous skeleton filled the hallway, scraping the walls.

Everyone turned as it lowered its head to attack and came rattling on its three skeletal legs, closing in rapidly on the mummy.

"Have a good meal!" Slappy shouted to the tall dinosaur skeleton. *"I hope he isn't too dry for you! Hahaha."*

31

The mummy staggered back, eyes on the dinosaur's massive snapping jaws high above his head.

The dinosaur threw a deep shadow over the floor, over all of us, as it moved. Balancing on its three legs, it tossed its head high. Then opened its jaws wide and zoomed down to feed.

Arragotus raised a fist—and slammed it hard into the dinosaur's open jaw. A powerful punch that sent a *craaaaack* that echoed off the walls.

The jawbone fell off and hit the floor, bouncing to the wall.

Arragotus landed another punch—and the head flew off. The rib bones clattered free. The leg bones collapsed.

In seconds, the dinosaur crumbled to pieces. The bones fell in a heap on the floor, rattling noisily.

With a roar, the mummy raised his fists in triumph.

"Oops!" Slappy cried. *"I guess dinosaur dinnertime will have to be postponed!"*

The mummy turned to Slappy. He reached out for him, but I moved fast. I dove forward and lifted the dummy off the floor. Then I turned and ran, carrying him in front of me to the far end of the room.

"Can't you *do* something?" I pleaded. "You're supposed to have powers. Can't you defeat the mummy? Isn't there something you can do?"

Slappy blinked his eyes. He tilted his head to one side. He gazed at the shelf behind us. *"Well . . . I have one more idea."*

32

Slappy stared at the shelf, at the pile of amber stones that Shannon had stacked there. He raised both arms and began to chant. I couldn't hear the words. His voice was a whisper.

Slappy continued to wave both hands at the stones, murmuring the same string of words over and over.

As I stared in confusion, the amber stones began to move. They popped open silently. The amber appeared to melt. Bubbles formed and the stones oozed onto the shelf.

And then I realized what Slappy was doing.

The insects . . . the ancient insects . . . thousands of years old. They'd been trapped so long, and now he was setting them free.

Their spindly legs quivered. Antennae waved above their sleek heads for the first time in two thousand years. Paper-thin wings fluttered. Round black eyes rolled.

The insects breathed and wriggled and then walked. I watched them climb out from their melting amber prisons.

Over a hundred of them! They walked unsteadily, moving in narrow circles. They bumped each other and buzzed and flapped their wings.

"*Aroooo! Arooo!*" Slappy suddenly shouted. He motioned with both hands. "*Aroo! Aroo!*" He waved toward the mummy.

And as he shouted, the ancient insects obeyed. They huddled together. Formed a dark cloud of buzzing, biting, breathing creatures.

"*Arooo! Arooo!*"

Hearing Slappy's call, they raised themselves off the shelf. Swooped together. Swooped together and flew at the mummy. Flew onto his chest. Swarmed over his head. Covered his arms, his hands.

Buzzing and biting. Tearing at the bandages. Scratching at the thick, hard tar. Snapping and beating their ancient wings against him. Burying him. Swallowing him up in a deafening attack.

The mummy appeared helpless against the swarming insects. As they smothered him, the buzzing grew louder till it sounded like an angry alarm, till it drowned out all other sound.

Yes! I thought. *Yes! The dummy has finally found the way to defeat Arragotus.*

The mummy grunted and groaned. He slapped at his chest. Tried to brush the snapping insects off his head. He twisted and squirmed. He batted them off his arms, pounding himself hard with his covered fists. He scratched and swiped and tried to pry them from where his eyes had been.

I stared in shock as the tar began to ooze. The bandages frayed and came loose.

Slappy tossed back his head and laughed. *"Yes! I'm starting to bug you—aren't I?"* he rasped. *"You know what you should do? You should call for the exterminator! Because I'm going to* exterminate *you! Hahahaha!"*

Arragotus swung his arm hard—and sent a swarm of insects flying. I watched them land on Shannon and Aaron. They cried out and started slapping at the bugs that clung to their skin.

Another hard swing of his body and more insects flew off into the hallway. The mummy brushed them off his head, flung them toward us.

And as I watched in horror, everyone was battling the ancient insects now, pulling them from their hair, brushing them from their eyes. Screaming and struggling to dodge them.

I saw a fat, furry bug buzz into Logan's open mouth. His eyes bulged and he began gagging and choking. Kids battled the attacking insects. Arragotus brushed the last of them off the top of his head.

"Don't worry, everyone!" Slappy screamed. *"Don't worry! I'm going to save you kids—save you for ME! Hahahaha!"*

He was the only one laughing.

I saw Aaron pluck a big insect from his ear. Logan was still choking and spitting, unable to get the disgusting bug off his tongue. Dad was bent over, struggling to brush bugs off both legs.

"Somebody help!"

"It's biting me! Owwww!"

"It stings!"

"Help me—they're climbing up my back!"

Shouts and cries rang off the walls. Slappy tossed back his head and laughed again. *"Wouldn't you know it?"* he cried. *"It's the one time I forgot to bring bug spray! Anybody got a flyswatter? Hahaha!"*

I could see he had no intention of helping us. His sick grin appeared to grow wider. He was enjoying the whole thing!

"Slappy! Help us!" I started to move toward him when I felt a heavy hand on my shoulder. I tried to scream, but the hand slid roughly over my mouth, cutting off my cries.

The mummy acted quickly. With surprising strength, he lifted me off my feet. I had no time to struggle. He swung me over his shoulder as if I were weightless.

"Noooooooo!" I finally managed to yell as he held me there with both hands.

I bounced on his shoulder as he carried me away from my family.

"Put me down! Put me down! PLEASE!" I struggled and twisted and squirmed and tried to punch my fists at him.

But I knew he was too strong for me.

"Please! PLEASE! Put me down!"

33

The mummy was moving fast now. I knew where he was carrying me. To the mummy room. To his coffin.

I turned and saw Shannon running after me, her face twisted in alarm. She stretched a hand in front of her as if reaching for me.

"Stay back, Shannon!" I screamed. "Stay back! You can't help me!"

But her shoes pounded the floor as she ran closer.

Swinging me on his shoulder, the mummy turned to face my sister. He lowered his head toward her and growled a warning.

"Shannon—get Dad!" I cried. "Go back!"

"Put Cathy down!" Shannon screamed. "You can't do this! Put her down!"

The mummy appeared to stare at Shannon. For a long moment, he didn't move. Then to my shock, Arragotus leaned forward and set me down on the floor.

I landed unsteadily. Dizzy, I struggled to gain my balance.

Before I realized what was happening, the mummy's tarry hands swung around Shannon's waist—and lifted her off the floor.

"Noooooo!" Shannon's cry rang off the walls.

The mummy swung her over his shoulder. She punched with both fists and tried to kick him. But he didn't even seem to notice.

Behind us, everyone still struggled to slap and shake the swarms of ancient insects off them. And I glimpsed Slappy, standing to the side, laughing, enjoying it all.

"You kids are wimps!" the dummy shouted. *"They're not biting you. They're only* tickling! *Hahaha!"*

Arragotus strode rapidly toward the mummy room. My sister bounced on his shoulder. I followed after them. I felt totally helpless. What could I do to save her?

"They're only tickling!" Slappy shouted again from down the hall.

And then I saw a strange look on my sister's face. Shannon stopped punching and kicking. She raised her eyebrows and a weird smile spread over her face.

And then I watched her reach one hand down and brush it against the side of the mummy's head.

What is she doing?

The mummy slowed his pace.

Shannon ran her fingers against his face.

I finally realized what she was doing. She was *tickling* him!

The mummy stopped walking. His hand loosened around Shannon's waist.

She reached lower—and tickled him under the chin.

He pushed his head back and made weird sounds.

"Grrummmpphhh grummmppph."

Shannon curled her fingers and tickled under his chin again. Then she tickled the sides of his face some more.

"Hummmpphhh grrummmppph."

What were those strange sounds?

Was it mummy laughter?

He lowered Shannon to the floor.

She tickled his belly with one hand. Then two hands.

He appeared to double over. Yes, he seemed to be laughing.

And as I watched in total shock, the mummy was on his back on the floor. And Shannon was leaning over him, tickling his stomach. Tickling him . . . tickling. *Until he roared with laughter.*

I stood with my eyes bulging, heart pounding, arms crossed tightly in front of me. Watching Shannon's fingers as she tickled the laughing mummy.

And then Arragotus gave one last laugh, a

hard laugh that made his head and chest rise up. Then he dropped back to the floor and was silent.

He didn't move.

I waited . . . waited. Waited and watched, barely breathing.

Waited . . . until I was sure.

The mummy was dead again.

I lifted Shannon off the floor and hugged her tight. "You did it! You saved us!"

Dad came running and wrapped us both in a joyful hug.

"The Mad Tickler struck again!" I said, laughing and brushing away the tears from my eyes.

Dad gazed down at the mummy, flat on his back, arms pressed stiffly at his sides.

"I guess Arragotus needed something to laugh about. He hadn't laughed in five thousand years," he said. "All that roaring and smashing things and carrying on and frightening everyone. He just wanted a little affection."

"Hey!" a shrill voice called from down the hall. I turned to see Slappy waving his arms above his head. *"How about some affection for* me? *How about it,* losers? *I'm going to be needing your affection for a* long, long *time! Hahahaha!"*

34

"Is it safe?" Mrs. Uris called. She led her group back down the stairs. My family was scattered in the hall. Logan and Aaron were sprawled on the floor, backs against the wall, heads down.

The screams had stopped, but I could still feel the panic in the room. Thank goodness the vicious, angry mummy had been put to rest.

But now I realized we all had another foe to deal with.

Slappy wasn't joking. He was serious about becoming our master. The only reason he had tried to defeat the mummy was because *he* wanted to be the one to terrorize us.

Now he waved his arms for everyone's attention. *"Listen up, everyone!"* he screeched. *"Now that Kleenex Face is sleeping the good sleep, let me tell you how you will spend the rest of your lives. You'll be serving me! Hahaha!"*

I gritted my teeth. His shrill, ugly voice sent chills up the back of my neck.

Enough horror for one night! I told myself.

I knew what I had to do.

Tickling wouldn't work for Slappy. But I was pretty sure I knew how to put him back to sleep.

He was waving his hands in triumph, raving and ranting. *"You're the lucky ones!"* he cried. *"The lucky ones to have* me *as your master! Haha!"*

As he shouted and waved, I crept toward him. Walking on tiptoe, I moved silently, trying to stay in the shadow from the wall.

I knew where I was going, and I didn't want the dummy to stop me.

Squinting hard, I saw the sheet of paper on the floor at the side of a broken bookshelf. I kept my eyes on it as I made my way across the room.

You're going to sleep for a long, long time, Slappy, I thought.

My heart thudded. My legs were trembling. I had to force them to keep moving.

That sheet of paper seemed a mile away.

Could I get there? Could I read the words on it before the evil dummy did something to stop me?

With a gasp, I dove for the paper. My hands shook as I lifted it off the floor.

I raised it close to my face. Cleared my throat.

And shouted the words on the page as loud as I could:

"ABASEEGO MODARO LAMADOROS CREBEN!"

Struggling to catch my breath, I turned to my dad. "Wait. Are those the right words?"

EPILOGUE FROM SLAPPY

Hahahaha!

Was that a happy ending?

Maybe it's a happy ending for Arragotus. He'll be back on his feet in no time.

Looks like Arragotus and I will have to share the spotlight. Oh well, we can both have fun terrorizing those kids.

As I always say, "Two deads are better than one!" Hahahaha.

Does that make sense? Don't trouble your little mind over it. Instead, remember that I'll be back before you know it with another story.

After all, this is *SlappyWorld.*

You only *scream* in it!

SLAPPYWORLD #9:
REVENGE OF THE INVISIBLE BOY

Here's a sneak peek!

Have I mentioned that I hate Ari Goodwyn?

I guess I haven't mentioned it yet.

But I hate Ari, and you'll soon see why.

My name is Frankie Miller. I'm twelve. My magician name is Magic Miller. My story starts while I'm onstage in the auditorium in front of everyone at Han Solo Middle School in Barberton, Ohio.

As you can probably tell, I like to be serious and careful and accurate and correct. Those are all important for a magician—especially for a magician who is just learning how to do dangerous tricks.

I'm in a magic club with my friends Melody Richmond and Eduardo Martinez. And Ari. One reason I hate Ari Goodwyn is that he is *not* serious and careful. And there are two other things. Ari is a goof. And he's a flake. And there's no place for a goof or a flake when you are performing magic.

Our magic club meets every Wednesday after school. We study the history of magic. We read about all the great magicians of the past. And we learn how to perform new tricks.

We don't really want Ari in our club. He makes fun of us. He messes up our tricks. He has no interest in the history of magic. He has a bad attitude. And *that's* the best thing I can say about him.

The problem is, the rec room in Ari's basement is the only place we can meet. It's the only place that's big enough for us to spread out and try new tricks.

Also, Ari's mom makes the best chocolate chip cookies and the sweetest lemonade. She brings them downstairs for us every week and then goes back upstairs and leaves us alone.

So, what choice do we have?

We have to keep Ari in the club—even though we wish he'd go upstairs with his mother and leave us alone, too.

Anyway . . .

I'm onstage in the auditorium. Mrs. Hazy, our principal, has introduced me as Magic Miller. And I am about to perform the most difficult illusion I know.

I am about to levitate myself off the floor.

I'm going to appear to float off the floor and hang suspended six feet in the air.

Of course, it's an illusion. I can't really float off the floor. I admit I have tried it several times when no one was watching. But I quickly learned the hard truth. I don't have any special powers.

Everything I do has to be a trick, an illusion.

Some nights I dream that I can fly. In the dream, Melody, Eduardo, and I are performing a magic act onstage. We are wearing long red capes and holding magic wands. And as we end the act, our capes rise up behind us. We raise our wands in front of us. And we fly off the stage and out of the auditorium.

The dream is so real, I think I can feel the cool wind on my face. The three of us fly—like superheroes—across the starry night sky.

I'm always so disappointed when I wake up.

As I said, I'm a serious, sensible guy. So I'm always surprised when my dreams are so wild, so unrealistic.

Anyway . . .

I'm about to amaze everyone in my school by levitating above the stage.

It took a long time to set up the illusion properly.

I have a harness strapped to my back that no one can see. The curtain behind me is black. And I have a strong black cord that stretches up from my harness. No one can see the cord because it matches the curtain.

There is a catwalk above the stage. It's like a metal scaffold with a wide walkway. The catwalk is hidden by the curtain.

So no one in the audience can see that Ari is high above me. He is kneeling at the top of the catwalk.

The black cord stretches from my harness up to the catwalk. Up there, it is coiled around a big metal wheel. You know, the kind of wheel you wrap a garden hose around.

When Ari turns the wheel, the cord will go tight. And then, as he turns it more, the cord will lift me off the floor. It will look as if I am floating up on my own.

Ari will pull me up at least six feet off the floor. All he has to do is hold onto the wheel. Hold it steady so I appear to float. Then he will lower me slowly to the floor as the audience claps and cheers and goes wild.

It was hard to set up. But an easy illusion to perform.

Melody and Eduardo were watching me from the side of the stage. Melody flashed me a thumbs-up.

I stepped into place. I could feel the cord tugging at the harness hidden on my back. I made my announcement to the audience:

"I will now perform the levitation trick known only to a few magicians in history," I shouted. "Watch carefully. Without any props or devices, I will rise up from the stage and float in mid-air. Don't try this at home, kids!"

I thought that was a pretty good joke. But only a few kids laughed.

I took a deep breath and raised my right hand. That was the signal for Ari to start pulling me up.

About the Author

R.L. Stine says he gets to scare people all over the world. So far, his books have sold more than 400 million copies, making him one of the most popular children's authors in history. The Goosebumps series has more than 150 titles and has inspired a TV series and two motion pictures. R.L. himself is a character in the movies! He has also written the teen series Fear Street, and the Mostly Ghostly and Nightmare Room series. He is currently writing a series of graphic novels entitled Just Beyond. R.L. Stine lives in New York City with his wife, Jane, an editor and publisher. You can learn more about him at rlstine.com

Catch the
MOST WANTED
Goosebumps® villains
UNDEAD OR ALIVE!

SCHOLASTIC
scholastic.com/goosebumps

GBMW42

THIS IS SLAPPY'S WORLD—
YOU ONLY SCREAM IN IT!